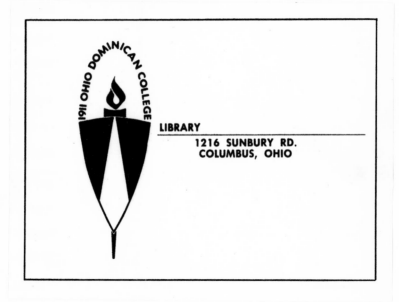

Chloris and the Freaks

Chloris

BRADBURY PRESS SCARSDALE, NEW YORK

and the Freaks

A Novel by KIN PLATT

J
P

To Lisa,
my sunshine, my love

1

I'm hooked on people and their birth signs. What my sister Chloris would call an astrology freak. I think there really must be something to this star business, and how the planets affect us, because so many times what I read in the newspaper astrology forecasts comes true.

Chloris is a Scorpio. Born under the eighth sign of the zodiac, the mark of the Scorpion. These people are very determined. They know what they want and try to get it in any way they can. Obstacles don't bother them because they have a strong will. The Scorpio is a positive person who enjoys winning.

That's the good side of the Scorpio.

The other side of Scorpio is not so hot. The Scorpio person can imagine injury when there is none. And being very proud, Scorpios can be sly when it comes to outwitting others. If they feel they have been done an injustice, they seek revenge.

Chloris scares me sometimes because when her mind is made up, she goes according to her plan and nothing can reach or stop her.

I happen to be a Libra. The seventh sign of the zodiac, the sign of the Scales. We Librans have to weigh things in our minds before we do anything. Librans love harmony and, generally speaking, are usually very sympathetic and also kind and considerate. They go out of their way not to hurt another person's feelings.

The bad side of Libra is something else. Insincerity is something we have to watch out for. Sometimes we want harmony so badly that facing the truth is too much and we make believe in order to be happy. Another bad thing about Librans is that we give in too easily even when we know we are right. We don't like to argue because it's too unsettling.

It's never any contest between my sister Chloris and me. Even if she didn't happen to be two and a half years older, she would be able to blast me down whenever she felt like it. She's that sure of herself and always has her Scorpion stinger ready to jab into people. By the time I think about it and decide how to answer her, the incident is over. Chloris is on to something else and I'm behind again, trying to catch up. It's good to be a level-headed Libra, I suppose, but with somebody like Chloris around, it's always a losing battle.

Fortunately there are a lot of other things and people around for Chloris to put down, and then it's more fun to be with her.

This day boys were on her mind.

2

"That Rick Harrison," she said, "really bugs me."

"Who's he?" I said.

"He's in my class. Boy, is he a freak!"

"How come?" I said.

Chloris looked at me as if I was dumber than usual this day. "Because he's freaky. That's how come."

"I mean," I said, "what makes him freaky? Is he some kind of nut?"

She nodded, her lips pursed. "Rick Harrison? I guess he's the freakiest kind of nut in school. In my class, anyway."

It was the beginning of the new school term so I still didn't know too much about Chloris's new friends. I was having a little trouble myself getting used to the changes. Different girls, different boys, different teachers. They really shook you up at school with all these changes every year, and it took months before you could get used to everything and everybody. Then by the time you finally had everybody all set in your mind, whammo—the school term was over and you got into a new class with a new bunch of kids, and the whole mess started all over.

I tried to think about the kids in my new class and if there were any freaky ones. There was a boy named Alec Bye. I liked his name, but that was all I could think of that was freaky about him. He was pretty bright for a boy.

"What do you mean freaky?" I said. "I don't know this Rick Harrison. Give me a freak type I know."

"Well, there's Alice Packer. She's freaky, all right."

I knew Alice. She'd been over to our house on slumber parties, just like Chloris had been over at the Packers. She was about the same age as Chloris, 14, but bigger all around, if you know what I mean. She wasn't just fat and heavy. She was really very well developed. Chloris was doing all right in that department too. Not as big but you could tell she had something up front. I've a slight problem there that I would rather not go into now.

I shook my head. "Alice Packer is always laughing and a lot of fun to be around. I always thought she was a good friend of yours. What makes her freaky?"

Chloris tossed her long dark hair. "Well, for one thing, she falls all over Rick Harrison. Putting out like that for one boy who's smaller than she is, well, that's what I call freaky."

I tried to recall if Alice Packer had shrunk any since the last time I saw her. I doubted it because she liked coke and tacos and tortilla chips too much.

"You mean he likes her?" I said.

Chloris glared at me. She has hazel-green eyes

and sometimes she can make them gleam. Maybe that's the Scorpio influence, too. I know I can't do it. I've practiced in front of the bathroom mirror and my eyes still look like regular dopey eyes no matter how mad I pretend to be.

"Well, I told you he was a freak, didn't I?" Chloris said. "I mean, if you fall for that jazz, you have to be an all-out freak type. If you ask me, those two freaks deserve each other."

"What do you mean she falls all over him?" I said. It was my Libra mind at work. We Libras like to get the facts straight so we can weigh them.

Chloris looked at me with her tired put-down look. "Don't you know anything?" she said. "She's always coming up close to him and betting him he can't lift her up."

I made a whistling sound. "Alice is pretty heavy. Can Rick do it?"

Chloris gritted her teeth. Since she had her braces removed, she can do it. I still have to watch that. "That's not the point, dummy," Chloris said. "Sure he can. But that's not the point."

I shook my head dumbly. "So why does she ask him to lift her?"

Chloris slammed her hand on the desk, bouncing her homework papers around. "To get him to feel her, of course," she said. "Don't you know anything yet, Jennifer?"

I shook my head once more. I always felt pretty

5

dumb anyway discussing anything with Chloris because her questions and answers seemed to be about things other than we were discussing. "Feel what?" I said nervously.

Chloris pulled a long face and sighed like a TV actress. She put her hands on her breasts and tapped them. She looked sideways at me. "You get it now?" she said sarcastically. "Alice is so big here that when that dope Rick tries to pick her up, he can't help but feel how big she is. If he doesn't watch out, one day she'll smother him."

I had to laugh. "That's gross! What do they do after?"

Chloris tossed her hair back impatiently. "That's all I want to talk about now. Blast off! I've got this homework."

"Gy!"

She mimicked me. "Gy-y-y!"

It sounds like the word "guy." We use it for words like gee, or gosh or golly. Chloris got me using it. A lot of kids in L.A. say "Gy!"

I went to my desk and looked around over my English homework assignment for Mr. Heartland's class. A book report on George Washington. He was a Pisces (February 19 to March 20) like Ralph Nader, Albert Einstein, and Elizabeth Taylor. But I couldn't concentrate.

I didn't know too much about how boys at 14 acted. The more I learned now, I thought, the

6

less surprised I would be later on. The kids my age don't do much more than pull your hair, or grab your books and run. After that happens a few hundred times, it gets to be pretty boring. All you can do is run after them and yell and feel frustrated.

Chloris had her notebook open, but her eyes were dreamy, staring out the window. I tried to sound casual about it, as if I really didn't care a lot. "How can you tell when somebody is freaky?"

Chloris thinks fast and talks faster. She grunted scornfully. "There are a lot of freaks all over the place. They're the ones who are really weird. They act far out, like they don't care what's happening. But they're really out to get you. You got to be pretty dumb to trust one of those freaks."

I shook my head doubtfully. "I guess I don't know any freaks."

Chloris smiled and smoothed her long dark hair. "Sure you do. We got one right here in this house."

That puzzled me and I had to shake my head again. "I give up. Who?"

"Fidel. He's one."

I stared. "Fidel? Our Fidel? He's a freak type?"

Chloris nodded and turned back to her homework. "Just think about it. You'll catch on."

I didn't want to think about it. After our father died, Mom married Fidel Mancha. He is an

7

artist and sculptor. But besides being a great artist, Fidel is a wonderful person. Always happy and cheerful, listening to you, making you feel important. Chloris was sullen when Mom married Fidel and wouldn't talk to him, or have anything to do with him. But she couldn't get his spirits down. Whenever he got me a present, he got one for her, too. Sometimes things she wanted very much. But because of her spite, she wouldn't use them. It had something to do with our dead Daddy but I never knew exactly what. Eventually Fidel's good nature got to Chloris. She didn't fall all over him but she didn't snub him deliberately anymore, and seemed to have accepted him.

Calling him a freak now got me mad. "You got to be kidding. If there's one person I can trust, it's Fidel. Even *you* like him now."

She lifted her eyebrows. "Do I?"

I forgot I was supposed to be a level-headed Libra and got even madder. My voice was shaking. "You're trying to spoil things again. How come you're changing?"

Chloris sat there, her nose in the book, ignoring me.

"You know he loves Mom and us," I said, almost crying. "He's no freak. He's a nice man. You're crazy."

Chloris lifted her shoulders, laughing silently. "Am I? You'll see."

8

I slammed my book covers together and stood up. I felt like hitting Chloris. But I knew that she hits back, and she's a lot stronger, so I had to be ready to run.

I reached out and grabbed her hair. "Take it back!" I said. Tears were coming into my eyes and spilling out.

Chloris slapped my hands away. "Cut that out!" She patted her hair back in place. Then she raised a finger and pointed it at me. "You think they're happily married, right?"

I nodded, my mouth open. Then I closed it and swallowed hard. "Sure. Anybody knows that."

Chloris lifted her chin and tossed her hair back like the girl does in the Miss Clairol TV commercial. "Wanna bet?"

I got close to her again. This time I was ready to punch her. "What are you talking about now?"

Chloris shrugged and stifled a yawn as if she found this all very boring. "What if I told you Mom was going to divorce him?"

I looked at her. My fist fell down to my side. I could feel my hand just hanging there, all limp. "How do you know that?"

"I heard her crying last night and the night before. If you want my opinion, she's had it with Mexicans."

I hit her then high on the arm. She jumped up and hit me back. Then I ran out of the room crying. I really didn't want to believe her because Chloris invents things a lot. But I knew now I wouldn't get much sleep for the next few nights.

I knew I would be keeping my ears pressed close to the wall that separated our bedroom from theirs. So I could hear if Mom was crying.

That's one of the strange powers my sister Chloris has. Even when you don't believe her, you're still not sure of anything.

2

Chloris began to change after our Daddy died. After the night Mom told us how.

"Your father is dead, girls. He shot himself. I don't know why he did it. Don't ask me. He didn't leave a suicide note."

Cancer is a word people don't like to hear about. I think suicide is worse. Cancer happens, you can't help it. Suicide you do to yourself. It's the final word.

That's what our Daddy did. Put a revolver to his head and pulled the trigger. He was 37 at the time.

I was five years old, Chloris seven and a half. I've thought about it since. Thirty-seven seems awfully young for a person to give up on the world. I know I could never do it. I suppose you have to feel awfully depressed for a long time before you can decide life isn't worth living. It must be terrible to go along thinking things will never get better and that you're better off dead.

After Mom divorced Daddy, he married Cindy. We saw him on his visiting days, and he would take Chloris and me out to his boat. If we scrubbed and polished it clean, he gave us each a quarter. Sometimes he took us out for a ride. I don't remember him being depressed. I try but I don't remember too much about that period. Chloris remembers, she says, and she tells me we always had a good time and Daddy was fun to be with.

Cindy was a secretary who had worked down at his office. She was dark-haired and very pretty. We didn't see her too much. Mostly Daddy alone on his boat.

I didn't know it but Cindy was pregnant then. And not long after he died, she had his son. Little Jeff.

This is the part I don't like about Daddy taking his own life. Didn't he think at all about his child on the way? Didn't he think about leaving Cindy alone? And what about Chloris and me? Didn't he think about us at all, and how we would feel growing up without him? And why not try to explain to us about this big problem he had that he couldn't handle?

I suppose that's the big difference between Chloris and me. She likes him more since he did it and I don't. Maybe it's the Libra in me, wanting things fair and balanced. If Daddy had asked me, I would have told him he didn't have the right to do what he did. There were other people to consider besides himself.

12

But I can't be too sure. I didn't know what his problem was.

Chloris and I had been playing in our room that bad night. Mom called us inside. She motioned toward the living room sofa without saying anything. Chloris and I sat down. Mom looked pale, her eyes nervous. She kept rubbing her hands. Chloris and I looked at each other wondering what we had done wrong.

The apartment seemed very quiet. I could hear the hum of the refrigerator motor. Night birds calling outside. Mom sat down on the soft chair and cleared her throat.

"Girls," she said finally, "I have to tell you something. Your father is dead."

Chloris and I looked at each other. At five, maybe I was too young to understand. I don't remember what I felt. I only remember looking at Mom, then at Chloris, and her looking back at me without any expression, then her looking at Mom.

Nobody cried. Not me, not Chloris, not Mom.

"The rest of it isn't easy to say," Mom said. "But you might as well hear about it now, and then perhaps you'll be able to forget it."

Chloris had her head cocked, turning her feet and looking at them as if she had never noticed she had feet before.

"A lot of people die," Mom continued. "As a

rule, they are much older than your father was. But he couldn't wait, it seems. So he shot himself."

I should have said something but I didn't. I should have asked her something, but I didn't. It was almost as if both Chloris and I were too embarrassed to say anything. We knew they were divorced, that she didn't love him anymore. Maybe she couldn't have acted any different, but if she had, then I think Chloris and I might have said something.

Then came the part about not asking her why, because she didn't know, because he didn't leave any suicide note. "Perhaps he was having trouble with his marriage to that girl from his office. Because I understand he's been living alone on his boat."

Mom got up. "If I hear anything more, I'll let you know. You can sleep together tonight, if you like."

The telephone rang. She went into her bedroom, closing the door behind her. We could hear her talking. She didn't sound broken up.

Chloris jabbed my side with her elbow. It hurt. She stopped me from yelling by putting her finger over her lips. "She's making it up," Chloris said. "Our Daddy didn't kill himself. He wouldn't do a dumb thing like that."

"But Mom said—"

Chloris shook her head, her eyes fierce and

gleaming. "Don't believe what she said. She hates him."

"But—"

Chloris pulled my arm, yanking me up. "Come on. Let's play a game."

I followed her into our bedroom. We each had our own bed. Chloris sat on the floor. We played with some straw sticks and a little red ball. You tossed the ball and tried to catch it while you tried to pull some sticks away without disturbing the pile. We could still hear Mom's voice. She was talking a blue streak to somebody. Chloris got up and closed our door.

"He wouldn't do a thing like that without telling me," Chloris said angrily. "Why would he do a thing like that?"

I shook my head. "I don't know."

She knocked the straw sticks and the ball away. "I'm tired of this dumb game. I'm going to bed. Good night."

I crawled into her bed after her. Chloris was turned away from me facing the wall. Some time during the night, I heard her crying.

As we grew older, Chloris became more attached to our dead Daddy. She built him up in her mind to something like Superman. I was only two when they got divorced and couldn't remember him at all in our house as a Daddy. The next few years I saw him only on the visiting day,

Saturday. Sometimes he had to skip that, too, and Mom would beef about it, having us all dressed and ready for him. Then he would call and say he couldn't make it. Chloris used to cry sometimes when we were with him and he spanked her. I remember that although she doesn't.

But after he died, she changed toward Mom, and never hugged or kissed her again. It was because of something Daddy told her, she said to me, something against Mom. But she would never say what it was. It was her secret, just·between her and Daddy, she said.

When Mom began to date men, Chloris wouldn't be polite and say hello when they came to the apartment. She called them creeps. And when Mom married Fidel, Chloris wouldn't talk to him. She acted like he wasn't there. Mom scolded her but Chloris kept her grudge and refused to change. She even mocked his being a Mexican, as if that mattered.

Fidel stayed cheerful, not letting it get him, not trying to change over. I found it very easy to like him because he was so kind. After the funeral, Chloris found out Daddy had borrowed on her insurance policy money, and not mine. I got a lot of money for college. This upset her because she always bragged about being his favorite. When she got over it, she acted friendlier to Fidel. Until this new thing started that she was happy about. Mom crying, wanting a divorce from Fidel.

It didn't make sense. Mom and Fidel seemed to really dig each other. They were always touching with their hands or bodies, looking warmly at each other, using loving tones when they spoke. There wasn't anything freaky there, just two grown-up people looking and acting as if they were in love.

No, I told myself, Chloris has got to be wrong. If Mom is crying, it has to be for some other reason.

Okay, I asked myself, like what?

Lots of things, I thought. Women cry a lot. You see it on TV all the time.

The trouble was, I couldn't remember Mom ever crying.

Yelling, sure. Blowing her stack over little things that didn't seem very important. Like housework chores.

Mom didn't accept excuses. You did it or else. The "or else" generally meant Mom yelling her head off at us. But just that, no crying.

I decided not to let myself get sucked in by what Chloris wanted me to think. I realized now she was up to her old tricks, starting trouble again, and I had to try and do something to balance it.

The first thing I did was divide my mind into two compartments. Up in the left side, I put the information she gave me, true or not, about Mom being unhappy with Fidel, and so on. The one up on the right side was going to be used like a filing cabinet, with the things I knew were true.

Now whatever happened, I could put everything in its proper place and not be confused and worrying about it.

I started with Mom and Fidel and put up there on the right side all the good things I knew about how they were to each other. All the touching, hand-holding, hugging and so on.

Then I took Fidel and put up things about him. How nice he was. Always cheerful, happy to see you, ready to talk to you even if you walked into his studio while he was working on one of his giant sculptures. Although he had exhibited in a lot of galleries and was considered to be an important and very gifted modern artist, Fidel never let on that he thought he was important or something special. Instead, he always left you feeling that *you* were the special and important one.

You're really swell, Fidel, I said to him in my mind, and I'm glad you're my new Daddy. If you ask me, it's Chloris who's the freaky one.

I wished Chloris and I hadn't turned down his offer to adopt us, at the beginning. Jenny Mancha would have been a nice name, I thought. As nice as Jenny Carpenter. But I was much younger then, and I let my sister talk me out of it.

Fidel was much older than Mom, middle-aged but very big and powerful. Because he enjoyed eating so much, he had a tremendous pot belly. But he wasn't really fat, just extra large all around. Like his laugh, louder than any I had ever heard, coming from deep in his thick barrel chest, sounding like thunder. Then all of him would be shaking, as if everything there was of Fidel Mancha went into one single laugh.

He was Mexican, born in Guadalajara, but a citizen now. There were a lot of Mexicans living in L.A., according to Fidel, almost as many as live in Mexico City. When you consider that all California was once owned by the Mexican people, all the land, the first missions, the big ranchos, it's not so strange.

They got pushed out of their land holdings eventually, having lost or being forced to sell their rights, and somehow they became second class citizens in the state they once owned. Fidel explained it to me once, not sounding bitter. He said every Mexican or Chicano knew his heritage and was proud of it.

After Fidel, I put down about Mom the things I knew about her. She sold perfume and cosmetic stuff in Bontel's Department Store in Beverly Hills. She was on her feet all day, and when she came home they were killing her.

Mom's not easygoing and relaxed like Fidel. She gets nervous and loses her temper. Traffic always brings out the worst in her, and she yells at the other drivers, calling them names. "Stupid jerk" is her favorite.

"Look at that," she would say. "Did you see what that stupid jerk did? He nearly drove us off the road." Then she would yell at him, "Stupid jerk!" Mom always made sure the other driver was far enough away before she let him have it. But she got it out of her system. It's not all Women's Lib with Mom, either. She says it to lady drivers, too. There are an awful lot of stupid jerk drivers around L.A.

Sometimes Mom gets embarrassed by her temper. Out here, the bus system doesn't work too well. The area is too large and spread out. So instead of waiting around for buses, most people here drive their own cars. A lot of these people are very old, 70, 80 and older. They aren't very good drivers. They go too slow or get in your lane and make you miss a light signal.

Mom flares up and yells out the window, the old "stupid jerk" treatment. Then she'll happen to notice how old the driver is. Her face gets very red, then, and she shakes her head. "Well, how was I to know she was such an old lady? She pushed me right over the lane. We might have been killed. They really ought to do something about public transport here."

I wished I knew what really happened between her and my Daddy before their divorce. She won't talk about it, but one time she was arguing with Chloris, and she said something about Daddy not loving her, and going with other women.

I remembered Daddy was only 37 when he decided to quit life. And suddenly I realized that

20

Mom wasn't as young as I thought, because she was past her last birthday, and according to the birthday candles on her last cake, she was 41. Well, it wasn't old exactly, but neither was it as young as I thought.

Not exactly young, I said to my mind drawer, only 41, but still pretty. Okay?

Maybe that's what she was crying about, I thought. The fact that she's in her forties. I heard somewhere that no woman likes doing that. I don't know exactly how I'll be able to take it when I'm that age, but I don't see what difference it makes as long as you can walk and do things, and not look feeble.

Mom's mom, Grandma Grace, is over 70 already, and that's really old. But Grandma still looks nice and she walks okay, although kind of slow. We always worry about that when we go shopping and have to cross a street. When we start, the green light is on. The green walk signal goes on at the same time. So off we go, and when we're halfway across, the darn bottom light starts blinking, changing to red, and it says: DON'T WALK DON'T WALK DON'T WALK! We get nervous then watching all the cars on either side ready to zoom at us and cut us down.

Grandma only laughs. "I'll get there," she says. "Those people in the cars will just have to be a little patient, that's all."

It seems to take Grandma about 400 years to

walk across the street. And all that time, there are those rotten stupid jerk drivers behind the steering wheels in their big cars, their feet ready to stomp down on the gas pedal, itching to get at us. With Grandma moving along almost in slow motion, it's a real hairy experience every time.

By the time we get to the sidewalk across, I'm so sweaty you'd think I ran a hundred miles. I don't think it's Grandma's fault for walking so slow. At her age, she's doing the best she can. It's the fault of the dope who designed those dumb WALK and DON'T WALK signs for the corners. Why do they start changing and flashing when you're only halfway across? They scare you to death.

Grandma is a Gemini, the third sign of the zodiac. The sign of the Heavenly Twins. Natives of this sign are usually bright and quick-witted. They have a lot of different interests, keep an open mind, and are always anxious to learn new things.

That's not exactly Grandma although most of it is. Queen Victoria was a Gemini. So was John F. Kennedy, and Bob Hope, Laurence Olivier and John Wayne also.

Chloris was next for my mental file. She was my sister, and I loved her and everything, but she was a pain a lot of the time. Perhaps all older sisters are a pain. Mom told me once how it was when she was growing up. Her older sister Joannie was smarter than she was and always putting her down. Maybe it was natural, a family trait. But to make sure I didn't leave out anything important, I put up in my right-hand compartment memory file the fact that if Chloris wasn't a real fink, she gave a good imitation of one.

For myself, I put down that I was 12 years old. That I liked Fidel and was happy with the marriage situation and the family being together just as it was. That I didn't want anybody to change it. I knew all the rest there was to know about me, so I didn't have to put that in any of the compartments. I wished I knew more about boys, and that I was a little bigger up front, and that I was able to say what I wanted to say right away instead of having to go over it in my mind a million times.

Maybe some day, I told myself.

3

Nothing happened the next few nights. Maybe I fell asleep too soon. But probably nothing did happen because, knowing Chloris, she would have got me awake to listen if Mom was crying.

Saturday morning was my appointment with Dr. Eaton, the orthodontist in Beverly Hills. I had just started with my braces and still hadn't got used to them. There were certain foods like barbecued beef spareribs you were supposed to leave alone when you wore braces. But I've this thing about barbecued beef spareribs and I forgot what Doc Eaton had told me on the last visit.

"I told you, you dope," Chloris said. "You snaggle the braces when you eat those dumb spareribs. Don't you remember what happened to me?"

"Well, sort of," I said. "Anyway, it doesn't matter. It's time for my check-up anyway."

"Yeah," Chloris said. "But now he'll know what kind of dope you are, especially after he told you, and I told you."

"I can't help it," I said. "I got no will power at all about spareribs."

"You got no will power, period," Chloris said.

Fidel was busy working in his studio, which is a separate wing of his old house in the canyon. We piled into Mom's Mustang and off we went.

Mom wasn't very talkative and stared straight ahead, tightly gripping the wheel. Her face looked pale and not too happy, but sometimes that's how she is when she has to go shopping or drive through a lot of traffic. She tenses up, as if it's an ordeal. Both Chloris and I don't fool around when she's in this ordeal mood. So we sat in the back reading off signs, noticing the weird clothes on some of the street people.

It's a half hour ride from our house to Dr. Eaton's office building in Beverly Hills. We were almost there when a big green car suddenly pulled out from the curb in front of a bank building. The car cut Mom off and she braked and honked her horn angrily. The driver then slowed down, and Mom had to brake again.

"Dammit!" she said. "What's that stupid jerk doing?"

The light was green as we were coming to the corner and we could have made it easily. But the driver of the green car slowed down and stopped and crawled along again, as if he didn't know whether to go straight or try a turn. At the last second, he stepped on the gas and zoomed ahead. The light had turned to red. And Mom started to cry.

I was about to ask her what was wrong when

Chloris jabbed me in the side with her elbow. I looked at her, surprised. She was smiling, with a gloating expression. "What'd I tell you?" Chloris said.

I didn't get it. The street was crowded, a lot of cars jammed with people trying to walk across before the light changed on them. I looked up at the red light, and then at Mom crying. She was wringing her hands now on the steering wheel.

"Gy," I said. "What's wrong?"

Chloris snickered and gave me that knowing, gloating look again. This time I got it.

"You're crazy," I told Chloris. "It's the traffic."

She bobbed her head, still smiling. "Sure. It's that traffic, all right."

The light changed. Mom shook her head and got the car going across the corner. She dabbed at her eyes with a tissue.

"That stupid jerk," she said. "He cut in without signaling. Nearly ran into us. Then he makes the light, and we don't."

"It doesn't matter, Mom," I said. "We got plenty of time."

She ignored what I said and kept driving, drying her eyes. I didn't get it. How could you get so upset that you would cry over some dopey driver, or being stuck by a red light?

Even if we were a little late, it didn't make that much difference. Dr. Eaton's waiting room

26

is always full of people with their kids. He has a good reputation, and fitting braces for kids' teeth in L.A. as they go into their teens is a very big thing. They all have appointments, like us, for months in advance, and Dr. Eaton is always running behind. We usually have to wait, sometimes 15 minutes or longer. It never was a matter of life or death. We weren't rushing to a hospital because of some sudden emergency. It was just another trip to our orthodontist over my dopey braces and Chloris's check-up.

Chloris was waiting for me to make the connection. It's got nothing to do with her and Fidel, I said to myself. Maybe a lot of people cry over red lights when they get stuck in traffic.

But I knew that wasn't too likely because it was crazy. And I knew Mom wasn't crazy, so there had to be another reason. Okay, she was nervous over something. Maybe she wasn't feeling good. Maybe she was working too hard.

I don't think you're even close, I told myself. But stay with it. You got a lot of other possibilities to go over before you get to the one Chloris wants you to think about.

Nobody cut in on Mom or made her miss a light on the way home from Dr. Eaton. She didn't call anybody a stupid jerk and even drove through the traffic as if she didn't think it was an ordeal this time. She was even happy-looking, maybe because Dr. Eaton said he could fix the braces I broke over those dumb spareribs. Without charging Mom extra money.

Chloris had her teeth cleaned and her gums stimulated. That's all part of the service deal you get at Dr. Eaton's.

"Look how white my teeth are," Chloris said, baring her teeth.

I nodded and showed her mine with the fixed metal braces.

"Ech!" Chloris said. "Go away."

"You had them for three years," I reminded her.

"I know," she said, "but I really didn't need them. My teeth were nearly perfect. Doctor Eaton said so."

"So how come he fitted you for braces?"

Chloris shrugged. "I guess it's the law here."

When we got home, Fidel was waiting in the house with a Bloody Mary all fixed for Mom. "Well," he said, "how did it go today?"

Mom smiled. "Everything went absolutely fine."

Chloris winked at me.

I knew what she meant. We both remembered it was not exactly as perfect as Mom let on. Now I had another problem.

Was she trying to keep that nervous crying stuff from Fidel?

So as not to worry him? Disturb his work and thinking?

Or did she have some other reason for not telling the simple truth?

I couldn't imagine why. I went upstairs to my room and lay down on my bed. I had a lot of things to sort out in my mind. I only hoped it would be big enough for all the little compartments I was going to need, to put everything.

4

Fidel's last birthday present to me was a neat "coffee table" book of astrology. I love it because it has a lot of pictures of famous people and their birth signs. Fidel is a Cancer, born under the fourth sign of the zodiac. The sign of the Crab, but also the sign of the Prophet and Teacher. Cancer natives are ruled by the Moon. It's a watery sign, patient, sensitive and sympathetic. That's Fidel!

The harmonious signs for Cancer are Pisces, Scorpio or Taurus. My Mom is a Taurus!

It's strange that although my sister is a Scorpio, she and Fidel don't get along. Maybe some day.

Henry VIII was a Cancer. June 28, 1491. Rembrandt—July 15, 1606. Thoreau—July 12, 1817. Also Ringo Starr—July 7, 1940.

About Taurus, it's an earthy sign. A Taurus is systematic, steadfast and kind hearted. That fits Mom. It's also the sign of the Bull. Mom doesn't like to hear that. She won't admit she is very stubborn, bullheaded and obstinate like a lot of Taureans. But her ruler is Venus, and she likes that. Her birthday is May 13th.

30

Catherine the Great was a Taurus. May 2, 1729. Queen Elizabeth II—April 22. Barbra Streisand—April 24.

The harmonious signs for Mom and the other Taurus natives for business, marriage or companionship are Capricorn, Virgo and Cancer. No matter what Chloris says, I know Fidel and Mom are good harmonious signs.

My Daddy was a Virgo. Although that is supposed to be a good sign for Taurus, some Virgos are very fussy and hard to live with. They're the perfectionists of the zodiac system. Maybe that's why Mom and he broke up. You don't have to take astrology seriously as I do, but if you think about one person who wanted things just so, like my Daddy, and another person who was so stubborn she wouldn't give in, then what you have is a harmonious arrangement that doesn't work, and ends in a divorce.

The Virgos are the sixth sign of the zodiac, the sign of the Critic. Greta Garbo is one. Also Ingrid Bergman, Lauren Bacall and Sophia Loren, Lyndon Johnson and Peter Sellers.

I told Chloris once about some other Librans beside me who were famous. Eleanor Roosevelt. Julie Andrews and Brigitte Bardot. John Lennon. Also Charlie Brown, whose birthday is October 1st. Chloris looked through my book and picked out Scorpios like herself who were famous. Like

Marie Antoinette. Katherine Hepburn. And Grace Kelly.

I can't see Chloris anywhere near resembling Grace Kelly. Although I have to admit she acts as if she's some kind of princess.

Whenever our daily newspaper is delivered, I always turn to the section where they have the astrological forecast. It's written by Mr. Wilson Wood. Sometimes he writes about exactly what's on your mind and tells you what to do. Other times, he barely misses and the person with the sign following yours has the forecast you think should be for you.

I also get the astrology magazines monthly with my allowance and keep up with what's happening. In those, I find a weekly and sometimes a full month forecast. From what I understand about astrology, these forecasts are too general and apply to a lot of people. But I can't afford the personal horoscope which would deal directly with my exact time and date of birth.

The monthly magazine said June would be an exciting month for Librans, full of changes. Mars was coming over my Moon and I would have to exert patience to deal with unexpected events.

I didn't like that, and looked at the Scorpio forecast, for Chloris. It said Scorpio was being favored by the Sun. Mercury would insure fulfillment of present plans. An unexpected alliance would be formed.

I checked out Taurus, for Mom. Taurus was in for stress and change with Saturn hovering over. Now was not the time to go full speed ahead with personal wishes.

I looked at the page for Cancer, for Fidel. Uranus was in, signifying great change. Great care had to be exerted not to be discouraged by present events.

The magazine gave days that were variable, disturbing, disquieting or good. For the whole month of June which was just starting, I had 9 variables, 11 disquieting, 7 disturbing and 3 good.

Chloris had 11 good, 10 variables, 5 disquieting and 4 disturbing.

Mom had 12 variables, 10 disturbing, 6 disquieting, and 2 good.

Fidel had 6 good, 15 variables, 4 disquieting and 5 disturbing.

The variable days seemed to be a little good and some bad. Things like: *Be more careful with yourself; don't be self-destructive. Modernize your surroundings, add value to your property. Do not plan ahead without being sure of your facts. Details will be misleading.*

I put the magazine down, more confused than before.

Mr. Wood wasn't helping me any in his daily forecast, either. Libras would be upset if they expected people to keep their word today. Scorpios had: *Guard your health, it may be better to keep your celebrating on the quiet side.* Taurus had: *Take care when handling sharp implements; do not allow the monotony of routine work to get you down.* And Cancer had: *This is a day for sitting tight. Give yourself more opportunity to think things over before you take any decisive action.*

I decided to move back to my own room where I might be able to figure all this out in privacy.

According to astrology, we are influenced by the planets. But we are supposed to use some self-will, so that bad things don't necessarily have to happen. Like Saturn, it's always a bummer, hanging over you like some dark cloud. You become very depressed when under the influence of Saturn, and to overcome this you have to try to be more cheerful. Mars is not so hot either, at times. It makes you very tense and aggressive. In that case, you must take special care not to blow your stack. When Venus is over, you feel warm and lovable. Jupiter brings you luck. Mercury helps you think better. Neptune can be good or bad. Sometimes it's very good for ideas and hunches, and making you feel like dancing or singing. It's not good for love affairs and other partnerships. Pluto brings upheavals and also new starts. Uranus is the same, even worse, sending a tendency to be "off with the old and on with the new."

I had to watch out for that Uranus!

The Sun is the most important and positive

influence. It gives power and vitality and self-expression. Without the actual sun, nothing would grow. It's very important to have this power in your sign and in the Fifth house where it should be.

The Moon has no light of its own and only can reflect the powerful light of the Sun. So the Moon is considered a sign which makes people responsive. Cancer people are ruled by the Moon in their Fourth house.

Like Mom, I have Venus for the ruler of my Libra sign. Venus brings love of harmony and a desire for happy conditions and relationships. Maybe that's why Mom and I get along so well.

My favorite metal, of Venus, is copper. My colors are blues and pinks. I'm a positive air sign. And later in life I can expect to have trouble with my kidneys.

Chloris is ruled by Mars. She's a fixed water sign. Her metal is iron, from Mars and Pluto. Her favorite color is supposed to be deep red but she likes green. She will have a tendency to rheumatism and trouble with her sex glands.

According to my astrology book, some occupations for Scorpio are butcher, coroner, detective, pharmacist, psychologist and public analyst. Because she is connected with Pluto, she can also be a sanitary inspector, a surgeon and an undertaker.

Chloris says this is all bull and she will be a

famous actress on TV and in the movies. She will also do a lot of hair commercials and toothpaste commercials.

I go with the last two because she is very pretty and has good teeth and a nice mouth.

As a Libra, I can expect to be an artist, beauty specialist, diplomat, general, juggler (for balance), staff officer and a valuer. Because of the Venus influence, I am strong in affection, beauty in shape or form (that's what it says), marriage and partnerships.

According to my sign, when the Moon is in Libra, the days are full of harmony and agreement. Relationships are good and hopes are shared. And love becomes the greatest. I get good cooperation at this time, and when I get married I'm supposed to do it at this time as then I face the prospect of a happy union.

The Moon takes 28½ days to circle the earth and the Zodiac. It spends only 2¼ days in each sign. During the time it's in Libra, I'm lucky. When it's in a sign not related to mine, things aren't too good for me. But it has to change signs again within 55 hours, and after that things can look better. And when it's in one of the signs I get along with, things are pretty okay.

That's about all I know about astrology. Because my harmonious signs are Aquarius and Gemini, you can see I have three chances every month to help with my special talent for marriage and partnerships.

That's better than nothing.

5

"How come you're moving back to your room?"
Chloris said.

"I just feel like it."

She smirked. "I know. You're afraid to hear it."

"Hear what?"

"You know—Mom crying at night."

"I haven't heard it yet," I said. "Maybe you're
only imagining it."

Chloris tossed her hair. "I didn't say it happened
every night."

"Anyway," I said, "I got a lot of studying to
do. So I'm better off in my own room."

She shrugged and lifted her nose. "Suit yourself.
I don't mind having my own room to myself either,
you know."

I hoped I wouldn't be sorry. Although Chloris
can be a real pain in the neck, she also is a lot
of fun at times. Also I wasn't too keen about
missing out on all the latest with her boy friends,
freaky or not. But it didn't have to be permanent,
I knew. And it wasn't like I was moving to Siberia,
but only across the big upstairs hall.

Even so, I felt sad about it.

Fidel helped me move my bed and desk into my old room. I carried the small stuff, the lamps and pillows. I told him where I wanted everything put. He was very patient and made sure everything was exactly where I wanted it.

"You and your sister not getting along?" he said.

"Not exactly. I just decided I wanted to be by myself, Fidel."

"Sometimes that's better," he said. "You know, this is a very big house. A lot of rooms. There is the spare room down the hall. If you like, I can fix that one up for you. It's even farther away from your sister Chloris, if that's what you want for now."

I flopped down on my bed. "No, this is okay. Honest."

He leaned over and rumpled my hair gently. "All right, then. If you change your mind, and decide to move back in with her, you let me know. Okay?"

"Okay, Fidel."

He was about to go out when I said, "Fidel, what happened with your other marriage? How come it broke up?"

He turned, surprised. "People get divorced for many reasons. It's not something one likes to talk about. It's all over. I try to forget it. Why would it interest you?"

"Just curious," I said. "Like, whose fault was it—the divorce, I mean—yours or hers?"

Fidel shrugged, looking unhappy. "It's hard to say after all these years. Fortunately we are blessed with the ability to forget pain. The memory fades with time."

I didn't get it. "You mean you still think about her?"

Fidel sighed. He looked like he couldn't believe so many dumb questions. He closed the door and stood there, his back against it. "A lot goes into a relationship like a marriage, you know. When you love somebody, you are giving them your life. And in return, you take what the other is willing to give. It's not something casual like merely living together. You absorb each other, your personalities. So when you break up, there are always memories. The other is still a part of you. You can't simply forget or wish it away."

"Then how come people can louse up something so important? I mean, what happens?"

Fidel came over to sit near me. "Did you ever blow a soap bubble? Hold it in your hands?"

I nodded, surprised. "Well, sure. A lot."

"Then what happens?" he said softly. "You look down and the pretty bubble is gone suddenly. Instead, there's only the empty place in your hands."

I thought about it. "Yeah. Like that."

"You were surprised, disappointed maybe?"

40

My head bobbed, remembering. "Well, yeah. Sure."

Fidel smiled. "You asked what happens with people? That's what happens. You look down at the shattered fragments of a loving relationship, and you wonder with the same feeling of surprise where it went, why it couldn't last."

I shook my head. "But that's different. Everybody knows a soap bubble can't last."

"You forget," Fidel said. "You didn't know that the very first time. Later, yes, you were better prepared, but still you had to be disappointed to lose the pretty bubble."

"Yeah, I guess. So you can't say whose fault it was?"

"No, not honestly. It's always easier to blame the other person, you see. So people lie to themselves. How can I admit that it was me, that I was a rotten human being? It's much easier to find the scapegoat—to say it was the other."

"Oh, you couldn't be rotten, Fidel," I said. "You're too good-natured."

"That's nice to hear," he said, "but remember, we're not married. Now I think you're a very nice person, too. But if we were married, you might press my good nature too far, and I might forget you were such a nice person. So many things could go wrong, and we would never be sure whose fault it was."

"I always thought there had to be some big

reason," I said. "Like my Mon got divorced because my Daddy stopped loving her and went with other women."

Fidel rumpled his hair. "Did your father tell you that?"

"Well, no—Mom did."

He turned his hands palms up. "Ah, but you have only her word for it. Before you know the truth, you would have to hear his side of the story."

"But he's dead!"

Fidel nodded. "Yes, I know that. But you have only your mother's viewpoint. You don't know the complete truth."

I couldn't believe what he was saying. "You mean she's lying?"

He shook his head. "Not necessarily. Not deliberate or willful lying. Merely her own version of what happened. But without hearing your father's side, you don't have the whole story. So you cannot form an opinion based on one-sided evidence."

I realized I hadn't ever thought about it that way. As a Libra, it was what I should have been searching for, too. I sat thinking about this, wondering how I would ever know both sides.

I must have looked very depressed because Fidel leaned forward to shake me a little. "Come on," he said in a coaxing voice. "I think this was supposed to be a friendly discussion."

"I know. But I'm confused. I don't see how

people can love each other so much, and then suddenly not."

"You'll never know the answer," he said. "That happens to be the mystery of the ages. Nobody has ever figured it out. But what you do is, you don't give up hope. You try again. You find some other warped being so you can start the whole nonsense all over again."

"How come 'warped'?"

He smiled. "I'm teasing a little. But I think you have to be a little sick or crazy, to begin with, to fall in love. To think that another is so wonderful, that you must have that or you can't live."

"Gy!" Fidel didn't sound very romantic about love.

He leaned over and patted my hand. "You know, I don't claim to be an expert on these matters. I may be the wrong person to be answering your questions. Isn't there a Miss Lonelyhearts in the newspaper? People write her about their problems?"

It was another feature column I read sometimes besides Mr. Wood's. *Dear Miss Abby,* she called it. "Yeah," I said, "but they write in about a lot of dopey things. Like what to do if the mother-in-law wants to hold the new baby. Should they let her or not?"

Fidel leaned back, reaching for his pipe. "I hope you remember what her advice was. Some day you may have the same problem with one of yours."

"Not me," I said. "I'm not going to have any babies. I guess you and your wife didn't—"

He surprised me. "We had a daughter, Jenny. Yes."

That was another thing I'd never thought of. Fidel having children from his first marriage. I'd never heard Mom talk about it. "What was her name?"

"Jessica."

"How old was she—I mean, when you broke up?"

"About your age. Perhaps a year older—13."

"Gy! Don't you miss her?"

Fidel's easy-going manner changed and his dark eyes glittered. I never thought I could make him angry, and for a moment I was frightened. But almost instantly, the dark hurt look vanished, and he was smiling again. The Fidel I knew.

His voice was soft but held a growling note. "What a question! Of course I miss her. How can you not miss your own daughter—someone you loved?"

He got up shaking his head back and forth, rumpled his hair, and then as he walked around the room, began to laugh. "Oh, boy, oh boy," he said. "Today you are uncovering the whole box of Pandora."

"Huh?"

44

He sat down near me again and took my hand. "Look here. I had put all these things—these old memories—out of my mind. To think about them again is like reopening old wounds. They don't hurt as much now, but are still painful. What is done is done, and you can't ever look back. Otherwise you can drown yourself in your sorrow, understand? It takes a lifetime sometimes to be able to forget what has happened."

I began feeling really rotten now. "I didn't mean to make you feel bad, Fidel—honest."

"I know you didn't. At your age, it's hard to understand what happens with people. But now that you've asked the questions, I can't hide. It's my own personal history, but perhaps you're entitled to know something about it, and maybe a little more about me.

"I was much younger then and didn't know too much about maintaining a relationship. My wife was young, too. We were the typical married couple, you see. Young, romantic, and very inexperienced. By the time we found out what it was all about, it was too late. It was all over."

"Gy," I said. "But you didn't have to give up your daughter, too, did you? Couldn't you keep seeing her?"

Fidel sighed and looked unhappy again. "We did that for a while, yes. Then my wife found another man she thought she could be happy with. I thought it would be better for Jessica to forget about me. To learn to know and love her new father. Otherwise, she would always be unhappy, wanting me and blaming her mother for marrying again. It was very hard on both of us, at first, but once I made the decision, I had to stick with it.

"I know at first she thought I had deserted her. But as the years went by, she overcame her disappointment with me. Her new father was good to her, and so, in the end it worked out all right."

"Gy, you and Mom are lucky—I mean, that you found each other."

"Yes," he said, smiling again. "Considering all the other people running around loose in the world, that was a pretty good trick."

"It's your stars that did it," I told him. "You got the right planetary influences. You're a Cancer and she's a Taurus. What sign was your other wife?"

Fidel sighed and rolled his eyes upward. "A Pisces. February 25th. I forgot to ask her before we got married. Was that a mistake?"

"No, it should have worked. Your sign does best in marriage with a Taurus or Scorpio or Pisces, like her. Unless you had Saturn over you all the time. How long were you married?"

"Fifteen years."

I shook my head. "Well, anyway, it should have worked."

"You can't depend on the stars doing the work

for you. You have to work at it yourself. Being married isn't easy, you know."

"How come?"

"The attraction, the tension, sometimes keeps people together. Sometimes it works the other way, and they wear each other out."

"What if they're just good and kind to each other, and loving?"

He smiled again. "In theory, that's very good. But without the tension, the conflict, a marriage can fall apart from inertia. From nothing happening to keep it alive." He frowned. "Like two vegetables. Then again, things happen. People change. You can't control things like that."

I hugged my knees up to my chin. "You mean you both changed, Fidel? I don't get it. You got to have some reason, I mean, if you were happy. Maybe she spent too much money. Or maybe your pipe gave her a headache. Or maybe—"

He shook his head, smiling again. "No. She was careful with money. She worked. She was a school teacher. And the pipe—no, she liked the pipe. She would fill it with tobacco. Light it."

He went on, seeing how interested I was. "It's only on TV that everything works out right for a happy ending, you know. If they showed life as it really can be, nobody would watch. They would turn it off out of boredom."

"You mean you got bored with your marriage. I mean," I added quickly, "both of you?"

He laughed again. "I think you'll make a good lawyer some day, maybe a good D.A. You don't let go. But you insist on a good sensible reason, and I'm sorry I can't give you any."

"I only wanted to figure out how it happened. Like with my Daddy and Mom. What if he loved her and then met some other woman and—"

Fidel shook his head and spoke sharply. "What difference does it make now? What your father did or didn't do shouldn't matter. Live your own life, Jenny."

"Well, it's hard to forget with Chloris, you know. She remembers more about him."

"Don't bother trying to remember. You can see how it has affected your sister. This strange allegiance to her dead father. She's a prisoner of the past, tied to his grave. That's sick."

"Well, she was taking therapy about that once, you know. With that Dr. Smythe, remember?"

It was very soon after Mom and Fidel got married. We all came to live in Fidel's big old house in the canyon. One night a fire in his studio nearly burned the whole house down. It burned a lot of his work, but he never said it was anything but an accident. Somebody careless with matches. Mom and I had a better idea. That Chloris started the accident. I think Fidel knew, but he never let on.

"Yes," Fidel said now slowly, "and she still needs help. She can't think straight about what is happening now. About what is supposed to be real in her life. That's why you have to forget, Jenny. Don't let it ruin your life, too."

He glanced at his wristwatch and I knew I was keeping him from his work. But I didn't get a chance like this often, just him and me talking together. I still didn't feel right about his answers to my dopey questions. But there was one left I had to ask.

"What you said before, Fidel, about your marriage—you made it sound as if it fell apart for no particular reason."

He nodded. "Well, you hate to admit that, that it fails and you don't know where to put the blame. Was it you, was it her? You want to know why, but there are no hidden meanings. Nothing lasts forever. It just happens."

"So you and Mom could get divorced for the same dumb reason—for no reason?"

He rubbed the back of his head. I guess I was giving Fidel a big headache. But his voice was still patient. "I don't know—so far, we seem to be getting along okay. We do our own work. We stand on our own two feet, don't lean on each other for support. We respect each other, our own ways and differences. Those are important things."

"What about love? Isn't that important, too? I mean, I know you do but—"

He laughed. "You want to see more romance? Maybe I'm too old. But you don't have to suck out another's blood to prove your love. You leave some, give the other room to breathe. You understand that?"

"Sure," I said. "That sounds okay."

Fidel laughed. "Don't be too sure. Sometimes a person is full of self-pity or self-hate and wants more than you can give. Then you're in trouble."

"Gy, Fidel, you make it sound as if you can't depend on anything."

"Well, that's putting it a little strongly, but it's not a bad way to figure. So you try to live each day and count your blessings."

I sat there dumbly staring up at him, not knowing what to think. He came over, bent down and kissed the top of my head. "You see, talking about divorce is always a depressing topic. That's why I try to avoid it. Okay?"

I nodded, unable to speak.

"Okay," he said, and walked out of the room. The door closed softly behind him.

I sat there sorry that I'd started the whole deal. I could see now that a happy marriage wasn't as simple as I'd thought. Fidel seemed awfully sure of his facts, and I wondered if my Mom felt the same way.

I was getting depressed. But I thought of Chloris trying to wreck everything, and got mad instead. I'm not good-natured like Fidel, and so right away I felt better.

6

Chloris came into my room mad. She slammed her books on my desk. Fidel had given me a lucky silver-plated horseshoe and it fell off the desk. I picked it up and rubbed it.

"What are you doing that for?" Chloris asked.

"I don't know. To bring back some of the luck, I guess. Anyway, if you're mad, why don't you slam your books on your own desk?"

"Don't be childish," she said. "How do you expect to make out with boys if you're going to be childish?"

"Who cares?" I said. "I haven't heard that you're so great making out yourself. According to you, everybody is a freak."

She opened my desk drawer, found a stick of chewing gum, snapped off the wrapper and popped it into her mouth. I had been saving that last piece for later when I finished my homework.

Chloris curled up the wrapper and tossed it on my desk. "You're not kidding about all those freaks. It's getting so that I'm beginning to think I'm the only unfreaky one around."

"How come?" I said.

She threw herself down on my bed and lay there with her hands locked behind her head. "Remember I was telling you last time about that freaky Rick Harrison and Alice Packer? Well, they finally got what was coming to them for all that freaky fooling around they've been doing."

"Like what?"

Chloris laughed and kicked her legs in the air. "Would you believe this? They were inside the supply room and somebody locked the door on them, and they couldn't get out."

"Did you do it?"

She giggled. "Maybe I would have, if I thought of it. Anyway, can you imagine those two freaks in there stuck with each other in a room no bigger than a closet? Especially with somebody as gross and fat as Alice Packer? I'll bet that Rick Harrison was peeling fat from all over himself when he got home."

I couldn't remember Alice suddenly becoming that fat. She was a little plump, maybe, but Chloris was slightly skinny, except for her bosom, that is, and I thought maybe she was just jealous that there was more of Alice Packer than there was of her.

"So what happened?" I said.

"Oh, they started banging on the door and hollering, and eventually somebody let them out. I wish I could have been there to have seen it. I wish I could have seen their freaky faces."

"Where were you?" I asked.

Chloris grinned. "In the cafeteria. Having a snack."

"Gy," I said. "But what were they doing in the supply room together in the first place?"

Chloris looked at me with her pitying poor-dumb-kid expression. She tapped her chest meaningfully. "Well, why do you think, dumbbell? I told you Alice was some kind of a bet-you-can't-lift-me-freak, didn't I? She probably saw Rick go into the supply room and figured she would put on her act, I guess. Anyway, she won't be able to get away with that kind of freaky act again, not there she won't."

"Why not?"

Chloris rolled over on my bed laughing. "Somebody made the school custodian take down the door. The principal, Mr. Beller, I guess. He's afraid of getting sued by those parents, you know."

"I don't get it," I said. "Why would they sue him?"

"Well, how would you feel if you were a parent?" Chloris said. "And your son got stuck in some room with an overweight girl. You wouldn't want that to happen, would you?"

"No, I guess not," I said. "Only what if—?"

"Oh, Pete's sake, forget it," Chloris said. She twisted around and rolled off my bed. "Let's talk about something else for a change. Have you spoken to Fidel yet?"

I looked at her guardedly. "What about?"

Chloris tossed back her hair. "You know what about. The divorce. Can't you see how uptight Mom is lately?"

"You mean about the traffic? That crying over the red light the other day?"

"No, dopey. About everything. Every time she talks to me, I get the feeling she wants to chop my head off."

"That's because you're a pain," I said. "It's got nothing to do with Fidel."

She shook her head and smoothed her sweater. "Gy, you are really too much," she said. "You don't see anything that's happening right in front of you. How much do you want to bet they get divorced before Christmas?"

I was so mad I couldn't think straight. "Twenty dollars!"

Chloris clapped her hands together triumphantly. "Okay. That's a bet. And when it happens, don't you chicken out of it."

I picked up my study book. "Don't worry, I won't. Now if you don't mind, I got this history book to read for tomorrow."

"Right on," Chloris said, swishing past me. "Only remember, that history is dead stuff. It's what's happening now that counts."

"Go away," I said.

"Twenty dollars," she said, "don't forget."

She went out the door and I slammed it behind

her. As a rule, Chloris is the one who slams the door behind people, not me. But this happened to be one of those times when she got me so stirred up, I did something before I weighed it over in my mind. I have to admit it felt pretty good.

I had been saving for a long time and had $86.32 in my bank account. I didn't like to think of it coming down to $66.32 because I happen to be very interested in money. But I decided it was more important to put my money where my mouth is, as some people say, and bet on Fidel and Mom not getting divorced.

I tried to do my schoolwork after Chloris left. I could hear her radio playing from her room next to mine but that wasn't what bothered me. It was the idea that she really wanted them to split. I couldn't understand that at all because Fidel was such a nice substitute Daddy.

It was strange, too, that she had told me history was dead stuff, that what's happening now is what counts. Fidel had said she was trapped by the past, by our Daddy's suicide and death, and I agreed with him. What I couldn't understand was how a person could be thinking two different ways at the same time.

I heard the phone ring outside in the hall. Chloris never answers it unless she's expecting one of her friends to call. Mom wasn't home and Fidel was in his studio. I let the phone ring, trying to outwait Chloris. But she won, as usual, and I had to go out after it. I knew the second I picked it up, she would be hovering outside her room asking me if it was for her.

It was my friend Kathy Kingman calling. She lives down the street. She seemed to be crying. I asked her what was wrong. She told me her folks were splitting, going to get divorced.

Chloris popped out. I shook my head, mouthing "It's for me." She went back in.

I asked Kathy if she was sure. She said real sure. I asked her how she could be that sure and she told me. Her father had left with his suitcases packed and gone to Texas.

"Texas," I said. "What's he doing in Texas?"

"He's got some kind of job there. Some instrument company. He works with computers, you know."

"Maybe it's just temporary, and he'll be back in a few days. That happens sometimes, you know."

"I don't think so," she said in a strained voice.

"Why not?"

"Well, they broke up a few times before, and he came back. This time, he's not ever coming back."

I said, "How can you be so sure?"

"Because I heard this last fight all the way through. Pop said he was leaving, this time for real. For good! And my Mom said, 'That's fine with me. Let's keep it permanent. Don't *ever* come back!' And he said, 'Don't worry! Never again!' "

Hearing this was a real blow. Her mother, Mrs. Kingman, is very pretty, about ten years younger than my Mom. Mr. Kingman was tall, and good-looking. Always whistling when he came home. Very happy, I thought.

"How long were they married, Kathy?"

"Next week would have been 13 years," she said.

"You mean, they broke up without even waiting for the anniversary?"

"I think they were both too mad to think about it."

"Does he have another girl friend somewhere?" I said carefully.

"Who?" Kathy said.

"Your father. Mr. Kingman."

"I don't know," she said. "How would I know? You don't think he would tell me about it, do you?"

"Not exactly, but I thought maybe your mother said something. You know."

Kathy thought about it. "No, it wasn't that. I think they loved each other too much for my father to have some other girl friend."

"That's crazy," I said. "If they loved each other, why would they want to get divorced?"

"Because they were always fighting," she said.

"About what?"

"Oh, dopey things. Like why did she have to put Crisco in the water before she made spaghetti when his mother never did."

"Crisco in the water? Why would she do that?"

"To keep the spaghetti from sticking together," Kathy said. "Her mother used to do it."

"So why did your father get mad about it?"

"He didn't," Kathy said. "Mom was the one who got mad. She told him if he preferred his mother's cooking, he could always go home to her."

"Gy! What did he say to that?"

"The first time it happened, he did what she said. He left and went back home to his mother." Kathy seemed to cheer up thinking about that and began to laugh. "But he came back in a week. He told Mom she could cook any way she wanted."

"Why did he say that?"

"I think he didn't like his mother's cooking anymore. Anyway, after that he kept his nose out of her cooking."

"So what else did they fight about? You said he left a few times, remember." I was trying awfully hard not to ask too many questions about personal things. But I also figured I had to keep up with what was going on with divorcing people, just in case the matter came closer to home.

"Oh, Mom used to empty his ash trays too soon."

I was puzzled. "How could she do that?"

"Well, he would be sitting there on his favorite chair, smoking his pipe, or cigar, or cigarettes. And Mom would always come over and empty the ash tray for him. He would start yelling, 'If I wanted the goddam ashtray emptied, I would have emptied it myself!'"

"What did your Mom say to that?"

"She told him to drop dead."

"Gy!" I said.

"Yeah," Kathy said. "He once stayed away for nearly a month over one of those 'drop deads' of hers. But when he did come back, they never did have another argument over emptying a dumb ash tray."

"That's terrific! How did they work that out?"

"He gave up smoking. What's new over your place?"

"Not too much. Is your mother crying over the fact that he left?"

"Well, not exactly. She was mad, at first. Then I guess it got to her, and she got real low. But she's okay now. She's just sitting there nice and peaceful, enjoying herself."

I wondered if Mrs. Kingman had found herself a new boy friend already. I know she's pretty enough. Just to be on the safe side, I asked. "How come?"

"She made herself a pitcher full of Bloody

Marys. She's had four already. That's her world's indoor record. She hates to drink because it makes her dizzy."

"You want to come over here for dinner?"

"No, thanks. I think I better hang around here in case I have to take Mom's shoes off and put her to bed."

"Okay, I'll call you tomorrow, Kathy. Cheer up."

"Thanks. Did you ever try a Bloody Mary?"

I told her no.

"I just tried a taste of hers. They're not too bad. Maybe you ought to keep some of that tomato juice and vodka around for your Mom, to make her a Bloody Mary when she gets divorced from Mr. Mancha."

"Why would she get divorced?" I asked, surprised.

"I don't know exactly," Kathy said. "Only everybody is, these days. It's what's happening."

7

Chloris made the rules, as usual. "I'll set the dinner table," she said. "You help Mom bring in the stuff."

The kitchen was hot, Mom's face flushed.

"What's for dinner?" I said.

"Chicken and rice. You can take the salad bowl in meanwhile."

I picked up the big wooden salad bowl. The lettuce and tomatoes and radishes were sparkling wet. "How come we got chicken again? You already made it twice this week."

Mom stared at me unsmiling. She pushed a damp lock off her forehead. "Because when I get home from being on my feet all day, I'm too tired to cook. That's how come."

I was going to tell her we could have hamburgers instead, and tacos. But then I remembered we already had those a few times, too, lately. I took the salad bowl in to the dining room table. Chloris was setting the plates and silverware.

"Who was your phone call from?" she said.

"Rick Harrison. He wanted to take me out to a movie."

"You're funny," Chloris said.

"I told him I was sorry, I had other plans," I said.

"Bring in the food," she said. "I'm too hungry to laugh."

Mom was taking the chicken and rice out and putting it on a serving plate. The drumsticks were hot and brown, the way I like them, sizzling.

"Kathy called me before," I said. "Her Mom and Dad are getting divorced."

Mom said, "Oh?" She handed me the plate and let go before I was ready to take it. There was a big crash. I jumped back. We looked down at all the chicken and rice on the linoleum floor.

"Gy, I'm sorry," I said.

Mom put her hands on her hips. Her lips moved but she didn't say anything. She put her hand to her damp hair, pushed it back and looked wildly around the room.

"Dammit," Mom said. "Oh, dammit!"

I dropped to my knees, to see what I could salvage of the mess. The linoleum floor was usually pretty clean.

"Forget it," Mom said. "Get the dustpan."

I couldn't stand the idea of all that yummy-smelling chicken going to waste. "It's not dirty," I said. I picked up two drumsticks. They were too hot to hold and I dropped them again.

Mom came over with some paper towels. She pushed me aside and picked up some of the chicken and rice and threw it into the garbage bag.

"Why'd you do that?" I said. "We could have eaten it."

Mom handed me the dustpan and the broom. "Because we're not animals, and we don't eat off the floor. Not while I'm working."

She looked so mad, I didn't argue. I got the slop off the floor. Mom leaned back against the drainboard, her face pale, trembling.

Chloris came running in, with Fidel towering behind her. "What happened?" she said.

"We dropped the chicken and rice," I said. "We had to throw it out."

Chloris made a face. "Oh, great! So what do we eat for dinner?"

Fidel walked over to Mom. She was still trembling, her hands to her face, tears in her eyes. "It's nothing to be upset over," he said in his softest voice. Mom suddenly burst into tears.

"I don't know what's happening," she cried. "I'm so jittery and upset lately. Dropping things—"

Fidel shook his head, smiling fondly. "Everybody drops things. I drop things all the time." He enfolded her in his big arms. She rested against his chest, sobbing full blast now.

Chloris nudged me with her knee. Her eyes gleaming with malice. I shook my head stubbornly. "The plate was too hot. It burned her fingers."

Chloris grinned. She bobbed her head up and down with that knowing smirk. I wished there was another drumstick on the floor to throw at her.

Fidel turned to us, his arm still around Mom. "I just remembered a good Chinese restaurant. You girls get dressed and we'll eat out tonight."

Chloris looked down at her jeans, then at him. "Who gets dressed to eat out?"

Fidel shrugged. He smiled and patted Mom on the shoulders. "All right. Then we go as we are." He took out his handkerchief and handed it to Mom. She dried her eyes, blew her nose, and handed it back.

"What's the name of this great place?" Chloris said.

Mom's eyes narrowed. She gave Chloris a hard look.

Fidel was cool. "Tom Foo."

Fidel wasn't kidding about Tom Foo's being a good place to eat. It was only about a 20-minute drive into West Los Angeles. The moment you walked in you felt that neat Chinese atmosphere so that all you wanted to eat was Chinese food.

Chloris studied the menu. "I'll have those barbecued pork spareribs," she said.

I wanted them, too, but I knew I couldn't depend on Doc Eaton fixing my braces again for free. I glared at Chloris and she gave me her look of innocence. I ordered chow mein instead. Fidel ordered egg rolls for everybody, and appetizers, little pieces of chicken baked in foil paper. Wonton soup and roast pork and snow peas and shrimp chow mein for everybody. He showed me how to eat with chopsticks. The secret is all in the thumb and forefinger grip.

We had green tea in little cups and fortune cookies. My slip of paper said: DO NOT GET YOUR HOPES TOO HIGH. I asked Chloris what hers was. She passed it across. I couldn't believe it. Hers read: YOUR WISH MAY COME TRUE.

"What's yours say?" she asked.

I lied fast, folding mine and throwing it under my chair. "It said, 'your dreams will be answered,'" I told her.

She held out her hand. "Let me see."

I pretended to look under the table. "I threw it away."

I asked Mom and Fidel for theirs. Mom's also said: YOUR WISH MAY COME TRUE!

I didn't like that. I read Fidel's: DECEIT AND FOLLY GO HAND IN HAND. BEWARE!

My hands were shaking. I felt Chloris's eyes burning into mine. I forced myself to look into them. "Rotsa ruck," I said.

Mom looked at us both. "Is something going on that I don't know about?"

I shook my head. "That was a great meal. Thanks, Fidel." Mom thanked him, too. Chloris was busy reading their fortune cooky papers. Mom glanced at her, annoyed, but Fidel leaned over and said something in her ear. Mom shook her head.

"I don't like it," Mom said. "I thought it was all over."

Chloris looked up and smiled blankly. "What's all over?"

Mom got out her compact. She looked at Chloris and her face hardened. "I didn't hear you thank Fidel for the lovely meal he bought us."

Chloris grabbed for another crumb of rice cake on a plate. "Oh, I wasn't finished, yet. Thanks, Fidel. You were right, this Egg Foo Yong is a great restaurant."

When we got home, Mom said she was going to watch some TV. I went upstairs with Chloris. She went directly into her room and I saw her take the little pieces of Fortune cooky paper out of her pocket. She pressed them out carefully with her fingers and put them into her desk drawer.

"How come you're saving them?" I said, trying to be nonchalant.

Chloris shrugged. "I don't know. I just felt like it."

I felt anger coming up all through my body. "Like heck!" I said. "You're saving them so it will work out the way you want. That they'll break up."

Chloris moved across the room. "I better put on my record player. I can still hear you."

66

I came closer, wishing I had the nerve to hit her. "You may not like him. But I like him. And Mom likes him."

Chloris put a record on. The Osmonds. Tonight I didn't feel like hearing them. She turned to me suddenly. "I know somebody else who doesn't like him. Somebody you forgot all about."

I backed up a step nervously. "Who are you talking about?"

She looked at me, her eyes gleaming. "Our Daddy. That's who."

I stared, puzzled. "Daddy—? But he's dead."

Chloris shook her head. In the past, she always got mad if I reminded her our Daddy was dead. This time she didn't.

"His spirit is alive. It talks to me. Just as he told me it would."

I felt cold gooseflesh popping all over my arms. "D-daddy told you that?"

She nodded.

"When did he tell you?"

"A long time ago. Right after they got divorced."

"You're kidding," I said. "Why would he tell you that?"

"Because he knew he could trust me. That's why. You know I was always his favorite daughter."

The same dopey favorite-daughter-jazz all over again. I hadn't heard it in years.

I pretended to be impressed and believing. I had to find out what she was up to. "Yeah," I said. "I guess you were. On account of I was so little."

"Maybe that was part of it," Chloris said. "And also, I guess he knew I always loved him more."

"Right on," I said. "What do you mean about his spirit talking to you. *Talking to you now!* Isn't that what you said?"

Chloris closed her door. She leaned on it, looking me over, as if wondering how much she could trust me. I could have told her. Not very much.

She went to her bed and lay down, hands behind her head. "That's right. Daddy's spirit talks to me a lot."

"Like when?" I said.

"When I'm alone. When I'm in bed. Sometimes when I'm asleep."

It sure felt weird talking about this subject. "Maybe you're dreaming," I said.

She shook her head slowly. "No, I can tell. Because he talks to me and I talk to him. I tell him all the things he wants to know."

"What things?"

"Things he told me he would be interested in, like how I'm getting along. Things like that."

"What else?"

"Things like who Mom's new boy friends are going to be, after he's out of the way. And when she gets married, all about her new husband."

"You're positively weird," I said. "Daddy tells you that?"

"Not Daddy," she said softly. "Our dear Daddy is dead now. His spirit talks. Like we agreed before Daddy died. That he would come back in spirit form and I would tell him everything that's going on."

I stared. It sounded like Chloris had flipped!

I got some control back. "Okay, so what do you tell his spirit?"

"Everything. Everything that's happened. Mostly now, it's about Mom and Fidel."

"You mean, you told him—the spirit, that Mom and Fidel got married?"

Chloris nodded. "Of course I did. I promised, didn't I?"

I looked at her intently to see if she was shining me on—trying to fool me. "Okay," I said. "So what did his spirit say after you said Mom married Fidel Mancha?"

Chloris closed her eyes. She took a deep breath. "Daddy's spirit said we got to get rid of him."

"Get rid of Fidel?"

Chloris opened her eyes. They fixed on mine. "That's right. It's the only way."

"B-but why?"

"You know why," she said. "Because she was Daddy's girl. So she wasn't ever supposed to divorce him and marry somebody else."

"Daddy's spirit told you that?"

She shook her head. "No, dumbbell. Daddy himself told me that. Before he married that dumbbell Cindy. Before he shot himself. That's why he did it, you know. Because Mom divorced him and broke his heart!"

I was stunned. With Chloris, as I said, you never can be sure when she's telling the truth. I tried hard to think way back and remember Daddy those times with Chloris and me out on his boat. After the divorce. But I was only a baby then. What could I remember?

"So if she broke his heart, how come he married Cindy?"

"Oh, he explained that to me," Chloris said. "He did that just to show Mom. To get even."

I could only shake my head, dumbly. I remembered what Fidel had told me. That you only could know the truth after you had heard both sides. I had heard Mom's side, and now I was hearing, for the first time, my Daddy's side. Fidel said the stories would be different. Each party blaming the other.

The trouble was, how could I be sure Chloris was telling the truth?

I shut off the Osmonds' record. Chloris didn't complain. She lay there, still and dreamy-eyed.

"Maybe you got a rotten memory," I said. "Or you're making it all up."

Chloris smiled. "Wait till I tell him about Fidel's fortune cooky. That'll make Daddy happy."

"Why?"

"He told me that's the way she operated. That's how she got rid of him. With that deceit and folly!"

I couldn't stop myself from yelling. "What deceit and folly?"

"Mom's," Chloris said. "Daddy told me she swore to a pack of lies to the Court in order to divorce him."

"I think you're weird," I said. "I'm going back to my room."

"It's okay," Chloris said. "Daddy's spirit doesn't like anybody else to be around when we're having a conversation."

8

I got up early to read the astrological forecast in the daily newspaper by Wilson Wood.

The first one I read was Mom's: TAURUS (April 20 to May 20): *If some new idea occurs to you that can make your future brighter, be sure to put it in operation without delay. Be wise.*

I read it over three times. I saw you could interpret what Mr. Wood said two different ways. One, if Mom thought of divorcing Fidel, that would make her future brighter. The other was, if she didn't think of divorcing him, but living with him and loving him, instead, then *that* would make her future brighter. I wondered which way her mind was going.

The way she dropped the chicken and seemed to fall apart when I mentioned Kathy's parents getting divorced bothered me. If she wasn't thinking about a divorce, why would it upset her so?

There's another way, dumbbell, I heard my inner voice tell me. She doesn't want a divorce. The very idea of having a new divorce is what upset her.

72

I sighed, relieved. That inner voice of mine comes up with some pretty good stuff when I really need it sometimes.

I ran my eyes down the column to Fidel's sign. A lot of people are afraid of cancer and don't like to see the word because it frightens them so. For this reason, Mr. Wood never uses it. He calls them Moon Children.

MOON CHILDREN (June 22 to July 21): *You want to make some needed changes but first gain the cooperation of allies. Avoid a person who makes you feel depressed.*

I liked that because if Fidel had a problem, I could help him work it out. It meant he had to stay away from somebody like my fink sister who could depress nearly anybody.

I waited to hear if my inner voice had some comment. It was asleep somewhere and took its time. Finally, it came up with this: If you tell him there's a chance Mom might want a divorce, that sure as heck would depress Fidel. And then he would want to avoid you.

Two-way thinking can really be a bummer sometimes.

I looked at what Mr. Wood had to say for Chloris. SCORPIO (Oct. 23 to Nov. 21): *Discuss your problem with higher-ups. Take time to study an important undertaking.*

I didn't like that part at all about the higher-ups.

Was it possible Daddy really sent his spirit down to talk to her?

I looked at mine. LIBRA (Sept. 23 to Oct. 22): *Plan how to have more security in the places that count the most with you. Invite influential persons into your home.*

Well, that was really groovy. It was just perfect for me and my problem. How to keep Mom and Fidel together. The trouble was, I didn't know any influential people, let alone getting to invite them home.

I looked at the last sign, just out of curiosity. I didn't know any Pisces people. The astrologer had this: PISCES (Feb. 20 to March 20): *Contact a bigwig you know and get the support you need. A good friend can be helpful to you at this time.*

That would have been a pretty good one for me, too. I could have used a good friend now. I looked at ARIES (March 21 to April 19): *You are now able to clear up matters with others that are intractable, so use your hunches as well as your good judgment.*

Now I was sorry I had read beyond my own sign forecast. Here was an Aries I never heard of who could solve my problem. I wished I was an Aries now instead of just a Libra who was helpless in a very important matter, and didn't know any influential people to invite home to help her.

74

My friend Kathy is a Capricorn. They're people who worry a lot. I read: CAPRICORN (Dec. 22 to Jan. 20): *Although one at home does not comprehend your personal desires, don't let that keep you from going ahead with your plans.*

This forecast would have been a great one for me. I wondered if Mr. Wood had somehow made a few mistakes in this day's column and got people and their signs mixed up. Maybe he had a rotten secretary, or she was having trouble with her boy friend, and couldn't keep her mind on her work. I decided that some day I would write Mr. Wood a letter and maybe get to meet him. It could lead to my getting a job as his secretary and I'd get to know all about my favorite subject, astrology.

I cut out the newspaper column and put it away in my desk drawer with the others I'd saved. I had to keep a record on what he told me, and how it worked out.

If Chloris hadn't said anything about a divorce, I wouldn't be worrying about a thing. Once you get something implanted in your mind, right or wrong, it can really bug you.

The whole matter could be cleared up in a minute, if I only knew the truth. The problem was, I didn't know how to get it.

It was Saturday morning. A nice sunny day. I thought maybe Kathy could give me some information about what goes on before a divorce, which would help me read the signs better. I called her and she wasn't doing anything, so I went over.

Kathy is about my age, only two months older. My hair is dark, hers light. I'm on the thin side, she's on the chunky. Even though she is one of those Capricorns, she doesn't have any of the worry lines showing on her face.

She opened the door. Her eyes were red. She looked like she had been crying.

"Come in," she said, "but we got to be quiet. Any sound my Mom hears, she jumps ten feet."

I looked around. She wasn't downstairs in the living room.

"She's upstairs," Kathy said. "Trying to sleep it off."

"Did she get drunk?"

"I don't know about drunk," Kathy said. "But she was really looping. She didn't know what she was doing or saying, after that fourth Bloody Mary."

I looked at my wristwatch. It was 11:00. I didn't understand how anybody could be sleeping that late.

Kathy seemed to read my mind. "Oh, she was up hours ago. She made coffee and a few phone calls and went back to bed with an icepack on her head."

"Gy," I said. "Do you think she called your father?"

Kathy's lip twisted. "Fat chance. She was calling

some guy she knows. She's not waiting around this time."

"But is she allowed to do that?" I asked. "I mean, your father just left, you said. Don't they have to get divorced first—in court?"

Kathy shrugged. "That doesn't take long. It's automatic these days. Mom already called her lawyer to start things rolling. She gets the interlocutory part of it in six months."

I licked my lips. "You mean, your father couldn't stop her, if he wanted to?"

Kathy shook her head. "Not any more. Not in California, anyway. They just ask for a divorce, saying they don't get along, and that's it. Even if my father said they did get along, it wouldn't cut any ice if my mother kept saying they didn't. The judge would just listen to her side of it."

I thought about what Chloris had told me. "What if your mother wasn't telling the truth? What if they really were getting along, but she said they weren't?"

Kathy thought about it. "It wouldn't make any difference. They don't give you any lie detector test. Your mother got divorced once. Don't you remember?"

I shook my head. "I was too young. Only two."

"Well, then, ask her. She'll fill you in."

I said, "What does this interlocutory you mentioned, mean?"

"That's the first half of the divorce. It gives

the people a chance to think it over. They can still call it off if they change their minds and decide to try again, as man and wife."

"Do you think that will happen?"

Kathy's blue eyes looked very sad and troubled. "Not a chance, Jenny. Mom really hates him this time. If I told you what she's been calling him, you wouldn't believe it."

It sounded like Fidel hadn't been kidding. "You mean, like swearing?"

"That and a lot of other things."

"But how can she hate him so fast?"

"How do I know?" Kathy said, annoyed and angry. "For all I know, maybe she hated him before. Maybe she always hated him."

"Can't you tell?"

Kathy looked at me. "You've got a mother and a—well, Fidel is like your father now, right?"

I nodded. "Right."

"Okay. Can you tell?"

"They seem to be getting along, to me."

"Maybe one of them is faking it," Kathy said. She was very bitter, and I couldn't blame her. She really liked her father, Mr. Kingman.

"Maybe," I said. "Only—"

"Only what?"

"Chloris said—" I hesitated a while. Then I had to get it out because Kathy was my best friend. "Chloris said my Mom was going to divorce Fidel."

Kathy looked surprised. "How does she know?"

I shook my head. "She never liked Fidel. Maybe she's just making it up to scare me. She still likes—she's still hung up on our old Daddy. The one who died."

Kathy and I have always told each other everything we knew. She said, "I thought that was all over. That she went to that lady shrink and got straightened out."

"That's what we thought. But now it looks like it's starting all over again. Only this time, it's worse."

"Like how?" Kathy said.

I slumped down in her practically-ex-daddy's big armchair. "Now she's talking to his spirit."

Kathy's mouth opened. She didn't say anything for a while. Then, "How can she do that?"

"How do I know? She says she talks with my dead Daddy's spirit, and she tells him everything."

"Everything about *what?*"

"Just everything. And especially about Mom and Fidel. She says that's what he wants to hear about, especially."

"How come? I mean, why, *especially?*"

"According to Chloris, he made this agreement with her after he and Mom got divorced. Before he shot himself. He didn't want Mom to have any new boy friends."

Kathy smiled. "It sure sounds like your father was hung up on your mother."

"I guess so. Anyway, according to Chloris, he was."

"But, if you don't mind my saying so, he was dumb," Kathy said. "How could he stop her from having new boy friends after they got divorced. That's why they do it, isn't it?"

I remembered the different men Mom had brought home when she was starting to live her new life, as she called it. I could remember only a few that she was smooching with, but until she met Fidel, there wasn't anything real serious that I knew about. There could have been some that she didn't bring home, that she dated outside, that I didn't know about.

But that was a maybe. Maybe she did, and maybe she didn't. Maybes can drive you nuts and get you nowhere.

"I don't know why they do it," I said to Kathy.

She frowned. "They're all crazy and dumb," Kathy said. Her voice got higher and stronger. "Honestly, grown-ups are so dumb, I can hardly believe them. When you think of all the dumb things they do—like my Mom and Dad busting up that time just because he didn't like her putting Crisco in the spaghetti water. Isn't that dumb? Or because she emptied his ash trays before he wanted them emptied?"

I wish I knew a few in my own life so that I could compare them with Kathy's. "Yeah, that's pretty dumb, all right."

80

"I remember another dumb one, now that I'm thinking about it. You will never believe this dumb one, it's so dumb."

"I'll believe it," I said.

"Mom's car once broke down and needed the service. So my father drove her and her car down there, and took her home. But when it came time to drive her back later that day, to pick it up, he got tied up with business and couldn't. Don't you think she got so mad she wanted a divorce over that, too? She said if he loved her, he would have canceled his appointment."

"Gy," I said. "Maybe my father was dumb, like you say, but if you ask me, your mother acts very childish sometimes."

Kathy nodded. "You can say that again. Like with this new guy she's calling, as soon as my father left. You'd think she would wait a little while. You know, maybe think about what I might be thinking. That I still love my father and don't want her fooling around with some new jerk. But fat chance! She only feels sorry for herself, and doesn't give a darn about anybody else's feelings."

"Maybe she's afraid of getting old, and thinks she has to work fast," I said.

Kathy shrugged. "I don't get it. She's not that old. She's a lot younger than your Mom. I could understand it better, like if your mother started looking around for somebody fast once she unloaded Fidel—she's in her forties, isn't she?"

"She'll be 42 next."

"Well, there you are," Kathy said. "They only have a few years left then before they really fall apart, I mean, if they want to grab somebody. You take a good look at some of these older divorced women, and you'll see what I mean. They scare me."

"Fidel's 60," I said. "He doesn't look very old. He looks good and healthy."

"Men are different," Kathy said. "They don't age so fast, or maybe it looks different on them. It's we women who really get the shaft when it comes to getting to look old too fast."

"Well, we're only 12," I said. "We don't have to worry about it for a long time."

"I don't feel sorry for her," Kathy said angrily. "Why don't my feelings count? Why didn't they ask me how I felt about a divorce? Two dumb dopey grown-ups acting worse than kids in kindergarten. They call themselves adults, but they got to have what they want or they go into a temper tantrum. To tell you the truth, even though I think your sister Chloris is some kind of nut, I almost feel the way she did."

"How do you mean?"

"About my mother starting to go out with other men, bringing them around here while I still love my father. If she tries any of that, I swear I won't ever speak to them. Maybe not to her, either, ever again."

"Well, maybe she won't, Kathy."

Kathy's eyes rolled. "You don't know her. She thinks she's in some kind of beauty contest with the rest of the women in the world. Once she got my father out of the way, she's going to have a blast, I know. She thinks he never appreciated her and there are plenty of men around who will."

"Gy, I'm sorry," I said.

"It's not your fault. I got to go up now and change her ice bag. Before I forget, about your sister and talking to your father's spirit, I think she's making it all up, just to bug you. She's got that kind of mean weird streak in her."

"I think so, too," I said. "If only I could be sure."

"It doesn't matter anyway. As long as your mother and Fidel love each other, you got nothing to worry about. I mean, providing neither of them does anything dumb."

She went into the kitchen then to get some ice cubes for her mother. I said goodbye and left. I hoped Kathy was right. While I was at it, I threw in an extra wish, that neither Mom or Fidel would do any of the dumb things that married people usually did, according to Kathy.

9

The phone rang almost as soon as I got home. Chloris answered it and looked disappointed. She saw me and waved. "It's for you."

It was Kathy. She was crying again. She asked if she could sleep over at our place, if it was okay with my Mom. I told her, sure, I didn't even have to ask. She sounded relieved to hear that.

"What happened?" I asked.

"What we were talking about," Kathy said. "She made a date with this guy, and he's coming over tonight to pick her up. I said I didn't want to see him, I didn't want to be in the same house with him. So she suggested maybe I'd be more comfortable over at yours."

"Was she mad?"

"Only if you call screaming, 'mad.' She said she had her own life to lead, and no damn brat of hers was going to stop her. Also if I didn't like it, I could always go and live with my father."

"Are you going to do that?"

"Are you kidding? He doesn't want me, either. He probably has his own life to lead now, too."

Kathy was really bawling now.

"Well, come on over whenever you want to. Maybe it's not as bad as you think. Your horoscope was pretty good today. You know, Mr. Wood's forecast in the *Times*."

"What'd he say?"

"I saved it for you. You'll see it when you get here."

"Okay. But can't you give me a hint?"

"Something about going ahead with your plans, even though somebody at your house doesn't understand what you want."

"Wow! I'll be over soon as I can find my sleeping bag."

I felt pretty rotten after hanging up. I couldn't see where any plan of Kathy's would help bring her parents together again. She wasn't a magician.

Mom wasn't around, probably out shopping. Chloris had her door closed, with the usual sign on it.

NO ADMITENCE. THIS MEENS YOU.

I remembered somebody else who might be able to tell me the truth about Mom and my dead Daddy and dialed her number.

"Hello, Grandma, this is Jennifer."

"Hello, pumpkin. How nice of you to call me!"

"Maybe you won't think so. I need some information."

"What kind of information? I hope it's not about having babies."

"No, Grandma. This is about Mom and my Daddy. Do you know why they got divorced?"

"No. As a matter of fact, I don't even know why they got married."

"You mean they didn't love each other?"

"Well, how would I know about that?"

"I mean, couldn't you tell?"

"Maybe you're asking the wrong person. Your Grandpa and I both told your mother not to marry your father."

"How come?"

"He wasn't making enough money."

"Gy, what did that have to do with it?"

"You don't know about money. It meant that if your mother's new husband-to-be didn't have a good job and enough money, then we would have to support them."

"Didn't he have any credit cards?" I said.

"I don't think so," Grandma said. "You can't get a credit card if you don't have a good job and aren't making money."

"But—"

"Why are you so interested in what happened a long time ago?" Grandma said.

"Well, a friend of mine—we were just talking—her mom and pop just got divorced. So I wondered about why Mom did."

"You'll have to ask your mother about that, pumpkin," she said. "She wouldn't like my butting in about things that are supposed to be none of my business."

"How long were you and Grandpa Paul married?"

She was silent for a moment, and I hoped she wasn't going to cry. "Forty-five years. If he hadn't died, we'd probably still be married."

"Forty-five years," I said. "Wow! That's a lot!"

"It takes a lot of guts and gumption to keep a marriage going," Grandma said. "Most people don't want the bother. It's easier to just break up."

I wondered if that was what happened with Mom and my Daddy. "My friend Kathy's sleeping over with me tonight. I bet she'd like you to talk to her Mom and Dad."

"I don't think Kathy can afford me," Grandma said. "My rates are very high. A hundred dollars an hour."

"Gy," I said. "Is that what you charge?"

"No, but that's what I'm worth," Grandma said.

"Well, anyway," I said, trying to sound enthusiastic, "things are pretty good around here. Mom and Fidel are getting along fine."

"I'm glad to hear it," Grandma said. "I hope it lasts but I'm too old to believe in miracles."

"Oh, you're not too old," I said. "You don't look old and you move just fine."

"Tell that to my knees," Grandma said.

"What happened?"

"I made a terrible mistake," Grandma said. "I got old."

Then she asked me if my mother was home, and I told her no, and she said to take care, and that Mom should call her sometime. "If she remembers the number," Grandma added, and then we said goodbye.

The doorbell rang. I ran downstairs. Kathy had her sleeping bag under her arm. "I decided to check in earlier," she said.

"That's okay," I said. "I guess you're anxious to read what Mr. Wood said for your horoscope."

She nodded. "That and I couldn't stand it another minute over at my house."

We went upstairs to my room and I showed her the forecast. Kathy read it carefully. "Maybe he knows something I don't know," Kathy said. "I don't have any plans. Unless you count this one, sleeping over here tonight."

She arranged her sleeping bag in my room and I got some records ready to play. "I just called my Grandma to find out if she knew why my Mom and Dad got divorced."

"What did she tell you?"

"Either she didn't know or she didn't want to say."

Kathy nodded. "Even when you find out, it doesn't mean you're going to feel any better. For instance, I told you a lot of dumb things mine did, right?"

"Yeah, some."

"But I never told you why they really got divorced this time, did I?"

"No. Well, not exactly," I said.

"No, I didn't. The reason I didn't was I was too ashamed to tell you, it was that dumb. It was so dumb you wouldn't believe it in a million years."

I looked at her. "Well, you don't have to tell me."

Kathy shook her head. "No, I got to. Because I can't believe it all by myself. Anyway, here's what did it. You know my Mom likes to watch TV at night after dinner."

I nodded. My Mom did, too. "Maybe everybody does," I said.

"Maybe," Kathy said. "But my father didn't like TV. He hated it. What he liked was doing crossword puzzles. He did the one in the paper every night. He did it while Mom was watching her TV."

I felt sad. Here was my friend telling me why her parents got divorced, and I couldn't even remember what mine did at all.

"Now get this," Kathy said. "You know that big armchair you were sitting in? That was his chair. That's where he read his newspaper every night after dinner, where he did his crossword puzzle. On that chair, next to the sofa."

She sounded so fierce about this, I didn't know

what to say. "It's very comfortable," I said. "Nice and roomy, and it feels good sitting in it."

"Well, you might think so, and I might think so, and so might my father. But that big chair next to the sofa is what caused the divorce."

I stared. "Huh?"

Kathy nodded. "That chair plus the fact that my mother sat on the sofa a few feet away to watch the TV across the room. You understand?"

I shook my head. "Not exactly."

Kathy sniffed. "Mom would say, 'Harold, why can't you sit over here next to me, while you do your puzzle?' and he would say, 'Honey, if you don't mind, I'd rather sit over here and do the damn puzzle.' " Kathy took a breath. "How does that grab you, so far?"

I shrugged. "Is there more?"

"Not too much. Then my mother would tap her foot or swing her leg while the TV was blasting on. Then she would say, 'I suppose you think I'm inferior just because I watch TV while you're straining your giant brain on a crossword puzzle.' And my father would shake his head, and take a long, deep breath, and say, 'No, honey. It's not that, at all. I don't have any feeling about your watching TV, either way. You can watch it all day and night, if you want to. I just happen to like to do these goddam crossword puzzles. I like to sit here by myself, over here, so I can concentrate better on the damn things. It's just a matter of personal preference. You like TV, I like this stuff.' "

"Then what happened?" I said.

"So this time he shook out his paper and got to working again on the puzzle, and Mom went back to watching the TV, swinging her leg, looking over at him once in a while. Finally, she couldn't seem to stand it another second. She got up, walked over to the TV, and snapped it off. Then she turned to him, and she said, 'You're more interested in your damn puzzle than you are in me. You haven't said a single word to me all night. You don't want to sit near me and touch me. You don't love me. I want a divorce!' "

"And what did your father say?"

"He sat there a minute looking stunned. Then he got up and went into his room. When he came out he was all dressed and was carrying his suitcase, hat and topcoat.

"Then he went across the room to his chair. He picked up his paper with the unfinished crossword puzzle, folded it, and jammed it into his coat pocket. He looked awfully pale. He saw me then sitting there, staring at both of them.

"He shook his head, sighed, came over and kissed me on the forehead. 'Be a good little girl now,' he said. Can you imagine? He's leaving, and he just kisses me on the forehead and tells me that!"

"Gy!"

"He picked his bag up and went over to the door. Then he said he was leaving, this time for good. And she said that was fine with her, and to keep it that way permanent. She told him, 'never come back!' He looked at her as if he wanted to clout her. 'Don't worry,' he said. 'Never again.' "

"And then he went away?"

"Well," Kathy said, "they each added a few more things. My father told her she was a typical dumb broad, she didn't know a good thing when she had it. And she started to yell and told him he was a typical male chauvinist pig!"

"What's that?"

"Women's Lib talk," Kathy said.

"I mean," I said, "what does it mean?"

"I don't know. Anyway, that's how they happened to get divorced. Now, would you believe that?" I shook my head. Kathy began to cry. "Not only are grown-ups so dumb but they're so phony. They tell us kids all the time to say that we're sorry, and make up. Then look how they handle things. They'd rather be shot dead than admit they're sorry."

She threw herself on my bed then, hid her face and cried. I didn't know what I could do. I couldn't think of anything to say that would make her feel better.

That's when a person really feels rotten.

92

Mom came back from shopping, and I told her about Kathy wanting to stay over. "Did Mrs. Kingman say it was all right?" Mom said. I said I guessed so.

"She's here now, in my room," I added. "She's pretty broken up about their divorce."

Mom bit her lip and pushed her hair back off her face. She does that a lot, like the girls do in the TV hair commercials. Only she doesn't shake her head and make it wave loose like they do, but pushes it aside. "Yes, I'm sure she is," Mom said. "Poor little thing."

I said I had called Grandma, and she had passed on a message for a phone call. "Grandma thought maybe you forgot her number."

"Oh, for God's sake," Mom said, angrily. "She knows how busy I am. She can always call me, if she's lonely."

"She didn't sound lonely."

"Well, then," Mom said, "I'll talk to her later. Now if you're not doing anything special, how about helping me unload these shopping bags and put things away. Where's your sister?"

"In her room. Sleeping, I think."

"Well, wake her up," Mom said. "Tell her to come down here and wash these vegetables. I'm too tired. That shopping just wears me out." She headed for the refrigerator with a package of meat. It fell out of her hand when she opened the door. Mom looked down at it. She didn't bother stooping to pick it up. "I'm going to my room and lie down. If your sister isn't tired from sleeping all morning, tell her I'd like her to wash and peel the potatoes, too."

I picked up the meat and put it away. Mom was too tired to thank me. I heard the bedroom door upstairs close, meaning she wanted to be alone.

Chloris wasn't sleeping. She was practicing some of the expressions the models use in the women's magazines. The look over one shoulder. The haughty look. The drop-dead look.

"Try knocking sometimes," she said. "That's why they invented doors."

Usually I'm supposed to knock twice before Chloris asks, "Who is it?," but she never bothers when she comes to see me. I told her all the good news about the vegetables and peeling the potatoes.

"Why can't you do it?" she said. "I just did my nails."

"I got company. Anyway Mom picked you."

Chloris rolled her eyes. "Lucky me! That means you'll have to do all the dishes."

"Mom didn't say about that," I said and got out fast.

Kathy was sitting up when I got back to my room, and she looked better. I told her Mom said it was okay for her to sleep over. "That includes dinner, of course," I said. "If you don't mind vegetables my sister washed."

"What's your mother doing—cooking?"

"No, she went to lie down. She's tired. She's jumpy lately, too, dropping things and crying."

Kathy smiled. "That still doesn't mean she wants a divorce. Remember, Chloris is the one who started the story. I wouldn't trust her."

"I don't," I said. "Did your mother cry and drop things before—before what happened?"

"My mother wouldn't think of dropping anything," Kathy said. "She's got iron nerves. How else do you think she can get rid of my father Thursday night and be dating somebody else by Saturday?"

"You'll have to go back sometime," I said. "We don't mind your staying, but she might make a stink."

Kathy sat huddled, her chin on her hands. "I know. I just hate doing what Chloris did. I mean, now I don't want to talk to any men my mother brings home, but as long as that's what Chloris did, I have to think of something else. I don't know what."

I picked up the astrology forecast I cut out of the paper. "According to Mr. Wood, you have a plan. Try to remember."

"I don't have one, I told you," Kathy said. "The only thing I can think of is running away. Is that a plan?"

"I don't think so. Anyway, it's not such a hot one."

"Okay, you think of one."

I couldn't. "Would you mind talking to Fidel about it? Maybe he could think of something."

Kathy shrugged. "Why not? I didn't do anything to be ashamed about. My Mom and Dad did."

I knocked at his studio door. Fidel was hammering away inside and didn't hear. "What's all that noise?" Kathy said.

I knocked again. "He's making something."

Fidel opened the door and looked down at us.

"Do you mind a little company?" I said.

His eyes flicked to Kathy, and he stepped back, waving us in. "A little company is always welcome."

It was Kathy's first time in Fidel's studio, and I could see her eyes popping. Everything he works on is so big, it's like being in the Valley of the Giants. Also because Fidel uses only what he calls found materials, things that have been used already, the place looks like a junkyard. But in between all the wood and wire and stone and tin are a lot of very beautiful things he made, cutting things up, hammering them together, sealing the metal with his glowing gas torch.

"Wow!" Kathy said. "This is weird!"

Fidel laughed. "You have the making of a first class art critic."

"Kathy has a problem, Fidel. Her folks, Mr. and Mrs. Kingman, are getting divorced. They just separated."

Fidel tossed his hammer on to a large messy work table. "It seems to be a spreading disease. I'm sorry to hear it."

"I thought maybe you could talk to her. You know, like what you were telling me. Maybe she won't feel so bad."

He nodded, looking at Kathy as she wandered off. "Sometimes talking things over can help. She's about your age, no?"

"Two months older. But her folks are younger—I mean, than you and Mom. This was their first marriage."

Fidel scratched his head. "Maybe if we work it out, I can open a first-aid marriage clinic." He waved his big hands. "Give up this art business."

Kathy was staring up at one of Fidel's big constructions. It looked crooked, going off in all directions like a giant plant gone mad.

"Why is everything so big here?" Kathy said. "It's like being in a forest."

Fidel laughed. "It's my vanity. An artist tries to create things. He is not God, and he knows it. But also he must try to be larger than his talent. So if you try the impossible, it's not such a bad feeling if you fall short a little. Perhaps I also feel better when I work big—that surely somebody will notice this. It gives me confidence."

Kathy walked back slowly. "Well, that may be easy for you because you're so big yourself. What about people like me and Jenny? What are we supposed to do when nobody notices that we're alive?"

"Size means nothing," Fidel said. "What you are as a person is what matters. Allowing yourself to be hurt is only a thought."

"Well, I'm only 12, remember," she said.

"Listen," Fidel said, shaking his head. "Nobody is so big that he can't be hurt. Everyone is vulnerable in his own way. When you're grown up, you'll have problems, too."

"Maybe it will be easier then," Kathy said. "I got this thing now and I can't do anything about it."

Fidel nodded, his eyes soft, his voice gentle and serious. "Being young or grown-up makes no difference. Nobody is really weaker or stronger than anybody else. Being a child is difficult, yes—it is a very helpless feeling. Now if you care to tell me your problem, we'll talk about it, and see if there is a solution."

Kathy saw she could trust Fidel, and began telling him what happened. I left them alone to talk and wandered about his studio. Every time I visited there, I saw new things. He worked very hard at being an artist. And no sooner was one piece done than he began another. The wood pieces were huge. Logs, big roofing beams as thick as telephone poles, railroad ties. He dragged them into his Ranchowagon. When he got home, he wrestled them into the studio. His paintings were as wide as the walls, reaching nearly to the ceiling, strange shapes with glowing color.

I headed for the giant wooden horse he had made for me a few years ago when he first got to know me. I climbed up and put my feet in the leather stirrups and sat looking down on everything. Sitting there always felt peaceful. Even though I knew that big wooden horse was something Fidel had made, it had a magical quality. I had the secret feeling that it could take me anywhere in the world, if I wanted it to. That in one amazing second, the wooden horse would leap out the window with one tremendous bound. In another moment, we would be racing up toward the clouds in the sky. Then we would be floating, feeling the wind, watching the world go by far below, beneath the soft clouds.

I saw Kathy waving at me. I patted the wooden horse and got down.

"Fidel agrees that I have a problem," Kathy

said. "He doesn't think my father is coming back to live with her. And if he tries it, he'll be too late because she's going to divorce him for good this time, whether he likes it or not."

I frowned. I didn't like Fidel to be giving up on Kathy's life so easily. "Maybe her mother will change her mind at the last minute," I said. "Maybe she won't happen to like this new guy she's dating tonight."

Fidel shook his head. He tapped his forehead. "The thought is what matters. That she would leave her husband. That she would not care about her child's feelings. She is thinking only of herself, you see, of her own frustration, and nothing can stop her now from acting out the fantasy of her new life."

I wondered if Mom would do something like that to Fidel and me. I had read all the zodiac signs, and I knew how obstinate those Taureans could be when they got something in their minds. The zodiac isn't kidding about giving them the sign of the Bull. "So is it all her mother's fault, Fidel?" I asked. "If Kathy told you everything, then you know how her father was just sitting there doing his crossword puzzle. He wasn't looking for trouble, or any divorce."

"That's one way of looking at it," Fidel said. "From what your friend said, yes, you might think so. That her mother is acting impetuously, like a child. Wanting her own way."

100

"Well, sure," I said. "Why can't she watch her old TV by herself while he does his dopey crossword puzzle by himself in his chair. He's only a few feet away. He didn't leave town to do it."

Fidel laughed. "Now we will look at the other side of it. You blame the mother? Yes, it is perhaps her fault. Now I will tell you how you can blame the father, as well.

"But first, I think we will all agree that they were both acting like children. Do we agree?"

Kathy and I couldn't have agreed more or faster.

"Good," Fidel said. "Now we will discuss what grown-up behavior should be. It is called mature behavior. It means to have genuine concern for other individuals, and very little concern for oneself. Except for the pleasure of enjoying the pleasure of the other person or persons."

Kathy and I stared at each other. We both seemed to know immediately that Fidel had put into words what we both wanted to know.

Fidel waved his big brown hands. "So, as an example, now we take the father. True, he wants to do his puzzle in his own way. He likes to do it alone on his big chair, where he is very comfortable, where he is all to himself, himself against the puzzle. It is not a bad thing to want. It is only bad if the father does not understand the consequences of having what he wants."

Kathy and I didn't quite get it.

Fidel smiled. "The father has been through the

situation before. He knows his wife becomes nervous when he does this. He knows although she is supposedly watching and enjoying her TV, she does not really enjoy it because she wants him right at her side, to be close to her while she watches. Perhaps she needs the warm feeling of the father and husband being close. Perhaps then she feels more security, or love. But the father of Kathy knowing this, and choosing to do otherwise, is pleasing only himself, do you see?

"If he had genuine care and concern for the feelings of his wife, regardless of the fact that they did not make sense to him, then he would forget about how good it was in his chair. He would forget about being alone and comfortable. He would give up all those feelings for himself, and sit with his wife because she needs him there, and enjoy the pleasure of knowing he made her happy."

Kathy thought about it. "Well, sure. I suppose you're right. But to do that, he would have to feel chicken, right? That she made him do it, or there would be a big fight."

Fidel nodded. "Yes. With some men, it would be a matter of pride or principle. To feel pushed into something that is against our character and nature seems wrong. So we resist. Our ego, our sense of self-importance will not let us give in. Let *her* make the change, or adjust to it, we tell ourselves. *We* are doing nothing wrong. To sit near her on the sofa, when I prefer my own chair, is giving up my honor, you see, my own dignity and importance as a person. I am self-sufficient doing my thing over here. I want her to be the same. It seems only fair. For me to give in is to be a coward. Yes, as you say, chicken."

Fidel tapped his head again. "But it is vanity that does the thinking! The real self, the real person of the father is buried, he does not remember any longer his own identity, so he must sit with his armor against the world, and not be bullied or pushed around.

"The mother should be aware of this about a man, that she cannot push him too far, make him deny his manhood for petty or selfish reasons. But again, if she could think as a mature person, she would not ask the impossible of him. She would let him have his chair and his crossword puzzle. She would not put clouds into a clear sky."

The sunlight streamed through his large studio window, making everything look bright and sparkling, even the junk. Fidel opened the door. Birds were calling softly, talking to each other, asking what's new, what happened last night, how's everything?

There was a light breeze and high up on the canyon ridge I could see the high wild grass moving like a flowing wave.

Fidel lifted his thick arms and took a deep breath. He leaned down to Kathy and touched her face gently.

103

"Forgive your parents, Kathy. They are both weak human beings, as we all are."

"Thanks, Fidel," Kathy said. "I hope they both drop dead!"

11

The school bus has a lot of stops to make in our canyon picking up all the kids. A few miles down the road, a lot of wise-guy kids get on. They were always pulling our hair. I guess you could call them hair-pulling freaks.

The bus was about half full when Mr. Williams, the driver, made his stop. I nudged Kathy sitting at my side. "Here they come."

"Maybe they won't bother anybody today," she said. "It's Friday."

"What's Friday got to do with it?"

"Maybe they're tired from doing it all week."

One kid walked to the seat behind us. I braced waiting for it to happen. My hair is long, just right for those dopey hair-pulling freaks. I watched out of the corner of my eye and was surprised to see him starting with Kathy. My mouth opened in sympathy as his hand grabbed at her blonde hair.

Kathy didn't flinch or wait until he had a better grip. Instead, she turned suddenly, and brought her school books down hard on his head.

"That one's for Girls' Lib," she told him.

He grunted, let go, and looked at her with surprise. He rubbed his head. "Hey, that hurt."

"Next time find another seat," Kathy said. "I've had it with this."

When we got to school, we went to science class together. Mr. Farrell looked seedy and his suit was rumpled, as if he had spent the night on a sofa.

"You kids can pick your own topic to discuss today," he said. "I had a rough night."

"I pick divorce," Kathy said, her hand raised.

Mr. Farrell winced and shook his head. "Try something else. That's all I've been hearing about at home from my wife."

"Is she asking for a divorce?" Kathy said.

Mr. Farrell yawned and scratched his head. "Not yet, exactly. But it's coming, I can smell it."

"Do you have a TV set?" Kathy asked.

Mr. Farrell nodded. "Of course. Why?"

"Do you want to save your marriage?" she asked next.

Mr. Farrell thought about it. "Yes, I guess so."

"Take my advice," Kathy said. "Get rid of your TV set."

Mr. Farrell smiled. He's tall and young-looking, and wears his hair long. "What good will that do?"

"Just try it," Kathy said. "That's why my Mom just dumped my father. If we didn't have TV, they'd still be married."

Mr. Farrell didn't know what to say. He looked at me. "What's your formula for a happy marriage, Jenny?"

"Same as hers," I said. "Those TV sets can ruin you."

Mr. Farrell rubbed his face, then the back of his neck.

"While you're at it," I added, "if you got one of those big easy chairs near the sofa, throw that out, too. They're just as dangerous."

Mr. Farrell looked at Kathy and me with wonder. "What's got into you girls today?"

"We're trying to make this a better world," Kathy shouted. "Less dumb grown-ups."

Mr. Farrell closed his eyes and put his head in his hands for a few seconds. "Maybe you've got something there," he said when he came out of it.

He asked some of the other kids if they had anything to add about marriage or divorce. Four kids admitted their families had broken up during the past year.

"Would you say having a TV set had anything to do with it?" Mr. Farrell said.

The three girls thought so. One of them, Shirley Rogers, said all those dumb commercials could drive anybody crazy. She thought people should stop buying the dumb tubes.

Mr. Farrell asked the one boy, Pete Semple, if he agreed. Pete said what we all were saying was crazy. Mr. Farrell asked him why he thought so. Pete said, because his father was a TV dealer. "We need the money," he said.

Anyway, three out of four isn't bad. That's as high as they go in the TV commercials, when they tell you how many doctors or leading scientists picked their product.

Mr. Farrel said he thought that was enough of that. He asked if anybody had any other ideas worth discussing.

"How about astrology?" I said.

Mr. Farrell smiled. "Astrology is considered a very inexact science, Jenny. Let's hear some other suggestions."

He waited and didn't hear any.

"All right, then. Let's talk a little about astrology. How many of you know your birth signs?"

Everybody's hand shot up.

"That's very interesting," Mr. Farrell said. "How many of you read your personal horoscope in the daily newspaper?" He looked around. Everybody's hand was up again. "That proves what I've always thought," Mr. Farrell said. "This is a very inexact science class."

"What sign are you, Mr. Farrell?" I asked.

"I'm a Libra," he said, "but—"

"That's my sign, too," I said, interrupting him. Now I knew why Mr. Farrell and I always got along, even though it seemed as if we didn't. "Your horoscope was very good today. It could save your marriage."

His eyebrows lifted. "What was it?"

I told him how if he could improve his plans, he could turn chaos into greater success. What Mr. Wood said. To contact all the key persons he could. And show he was definitely on the ball.

"Thanks, Jenny. But I don't see how that can save my marriage."

"We told you before," Kathy said. "Throw away your TV set."

"It cost $400," Mr. Farrell said. "I don't know if saving my marriage is worth that. Now I might go along with the idea of getting rid of my big chair. That didn't cost me anything. It was an anniversary gift from my wife's mother."

"What's your wife's sign?" I said.

"She's a Leo."

"No wonder you don't get along. Your signs don't match," I told him. "She needed a Sagittarius or an Aries. You had to find an Aquarius or a Gemini."

"Maybe next time around," Mr. Farrell said. "I'll keep that in mind. But I must tell you, that while it's all right to believe a little in planetary influences, you must know that stars are not compelling influences, but tendencies. Not with forces, so much as inclinations. With probabilities to think, behave, and feel in certain ways.

"The important thing to remember always, for those of you who take this stuff seriously, is that we do not have to respond. We do have our own free will. It's called a response factor. In other words, some people might respond differently to the same astrological forces or influences, as they might to art or music."

"But it seems to work," I said.

"Yes, at times," he said. "On certain people. For example, Buddha was a Taurus. So was Adolf Hitler. One can be stubborn in one's habits, as a Taurus. Or persevere in one's efforts to free oneself from habits. Different reactions to the same sign."

Mr. Farrell said that if we were all interested enough, he would spend some future time with us showing how we could cast our own horoscopes.

The kids liked that idea. But there were certain books and charts needed, he explained, and it might take a while before we could get started.

"Meanwhile," he said, "I'm developing a big headache. Why don't you all spend the rest of the period just reading, or whatever you feel like."

Some kid slammed his book shut and Mr. Farrell winced. "Except loud noise," Mr. Farrell said. "Don't do any of that."

Kathy and I got together and I told her I was thinking of writing Mr. Wood at the newspaper to get a personal prediction.

"What can he do about it?" Kathy said. "He only tells about what he sees in the stars."

"Maybe if I can convince him how important it is, he might send me the whole month in advance, so I could know what's coming."

"That's neat," Kathy said. "I'll write him, too. He might know if my father is going to lose his job in Texas, and have to come home."

Kathy's father is a Leo. Her mother, Aries. Two more harmonious signs that didn't make it. It had to be that darn TV.

I wrote my letter to Mr. Wood while Mr. Farrell was dozing in his chair. He woke up at the bell and I borrowed an envelope and a stamp from him.

Mr. Farrell gazed moodily at the blue ten cent stamp before he handed it to me. "You'll notice," he said, "that across the top it says, 'We hold these truths . . .'"

I looked. "Yeah."

Mr. Farrell shook his head. "Well, there you are. They don't finish the thought. For ten cents, nowadays, you don't even get a complete sentence."

On the bus ride home, the kid Kathy had whammed with her books took a seat far away from us.

"Maybe I'll miss that stuff after a while," she said. "But right now it feels good to see that hair-pulling freak isn't going to bother us."

"Who else do you know that's a freak?" I said.

"Right now," Kathy said, "all I can think of is my mother. The TV freak. The divorce freak." She looked out the bus window. "There's one more," she added. "My father—the get-up-and-go freak."

I could see where maybe my sister Chloris had a point. There certainly were a number of freaky people around.

12

Things began happening that week. I should have known when I read the astrological forecast in the newspaper. TAURUS: *Get secrets of success from those whose operations differ from yours. Know better what your employer expects of you.*

Mom came home from work smiling. "You'll never believe this," she told Fidel. "My boss promoted me. I've got a new job as Assistant Buyer."

"Congratulations!" Fidel said.

"That isn't all of it," Mom said, her cheeks flushed. "I'm getting a terrific raise in salary. Thirty-five dollars more a week!"

Fidel was drinking a glass of beer. He raised the glass to Mom. "Good luck goes together. I am very happy for you, Margaret."

"What's that mean, Mom," I said, "Assistant Buyer?"

"Well, I've been selling cosmetics and beauty preparations, you know. Now I'll be dealing with the salesmen from different companies, deciding what to buy for our store that we can sell."

"Terrific," Chloris said. "What's for dinner?"

Mom turned and flashed her an angry look, but then she suddenly changed her mind, and smiled. "I don't feel like cooking tonight. Let's eat out, Fidel. I feel like celebrating."

Fidel looked at his watch. "The celebrating is a good idea. But eating out takes so much time. I have a piece that must be done by the end of the week for a showing."

Mom frowned. "Can't it wait?"

"It is a difficult one to do. I need all the time I can get, to solve the problem, to finish the job."

Mom opened her bag and took out some money. "I'll treat!"

Fidel flushed and his eyebrows drew together. "What has the money to do with any of this?"

Mom laughed. "Oh, I didn't mean it that way. Come on, I didn't make dinner so I'll take you out to dinner."

Fidel thought about it, rubbing his leathery face. "Well, if it means so much to you, all right." He turned away. "I'll get my eating-out clothes on."

Chloris said, "I don't want to eat out. I'm too hungry to wait for all that jazz."

Mom said, "I don't know if there's anything here."

"There's some tacos," Chloris said. "And I can make salad, and there's milk."

Mom looked at me. "How do you feel about it?"

114

I wanted to go but something stopped me. "No, thanks, I guess I'll eat the same as Chloe. There's enough tacos for us both."

Chloris smiled. "There, you see? We'll be okay."

Mom looked disappointed. "All right. If we're back late, remember to turn off your TV."

"But you can't come back late," I said. "Remember, Fidel has this work."

Mom looked at me and I got the message that I talk too much. "That's Fidel's problem, Jennifer. Don't you worry about it."

They left soon after, and while Chloris was preparing the dinner for us, I sneaked upstairs. I had forgotten to check Fidel's horoscope. His said: MOON CHILDREN: *Meditate. Reach better agreements with the one you love and come to better understanding.*

I looked at mine. LIBRA: *A good evening for inviting bigwigs into your home and entertaining them royally. Be congenial.*

I saw I had to explain this to Mr. Wood soon. I didn't know any bigwigs. I looked at the forecast for the sign below mine, for Chloris. SCORPIO: *Learn more from higher-ups and be willing to exchange views. Don't waste time.*

I put the clipping back in my drawer, with the others I cut out every day. I didn't like what Mr. Wood was forecasting. Although Mom's was okay if it brought her more money, Fidel's sounded like there was trouble. I didn't like Chloris still talking to Daddy's spirit and exchanging views. She probably would be telling him tonight how Mom got a raise and a better job and make his spirit madder. Mine was a big nothing, like Mr. Wood didn't seem to know or care that I was part of the family.

I was asleep when Mom and Fidel came home. I found out the next morning they had gone to a movie too. Mom seemed happy about it when she was having breakfast. Fidel was already in his studio working.

"I shanghaied him," Mom said. "It's been years since we've been to a movie together. And with dinner out, it was like the old days before we were married."

I didn't say anything. The newspaper was delivered to our door every morning, and I had taken it in first. This time Mr. Wood finally realized I was alive.

LIBRA: *Handle practical problems objectively. See how to make your talents pay off more handsomely in the future. Don't be overemotional.*

Right on, Woodsie, I said silently. I'm playing it cool till you tell me different.

The rest of the week was kind of crazy and mixed up. Mom came home on time the next night and made dinner. Chicken and rice. The next night she called, said she had to work late, and asked if we could fix our own dinner. Fidel said he would whip up something for us, a Mexican stew he was

116

good at. The night after, Mom came home tired and asked Fidel if he would like to eat out with her again. He said he was sorry, but he didn't think so. He couldn't spare the time.

Mom's eyes flashed. "You don't seem to understand," she said. "With this raise I got, we can afford to eat out every night now. Don't you see?"

Fidel didn't seem to be too glad about this new opportunity. He said it was wonderful that she got the raise, but he couldn't spare the time to eat out every night, and that money had nothing to do with it. Also, he didn't like to eat out, he said. He didn't like having to dress up, and he didn't like the food in restaurants, and besides, all he was concerned with at the moment was working, not eating, either in or out.

Mom got in one zinger. "You're always working."

Fidel scratched his head and looked at her, puzzled. "This is a special week for me, Margaret. I explained about the show and how I am behind, and need all the time I can get for it. But if it were next week, or the week after, or the week after that, yes, I will always have to work. I'm too old to waste the time, and I must put it to use. My work is to create, and I am lucky to have the gift and strength to do it."

Mom didn't say anything. She pushed back her hair and let her fingers play with the ends. She looked steadily at Fidel as if she were still waiting for an explanation. But he had said it all. He excused himself and went off to his studio. I could hear him hammering away all night.

The next night, Mom called to say she was working late again and would we fix our own dinner. Fidel came in, whipped up some hamburgers and spaghetti for us all, excused himself and went back to his hammering.

I didn't like what was happening. Mr. Wood wasn't any great help. TAURUS: *Step out of that rut and into new activities that will give you a new lease on life. Your intuitions are excellent now.*

Fidel's was better.

MOON CHILDREN: *Study interests that mean the most to you to make more money. Plan for more harmony. Visit with friends and family after work is done.*

I knocked on his studio door. The hammering stopped and I heard him walking across the room.

"You are just the person I wanted to see," he said. "Come in."

He waved me forward and I saw what he had been working on. It was three big stumps of wood that he had somehow managed to link together. Each one was bigger and wider than me. The wood had been shaped and chiseled and sanded down until it looked smooth. The figures looked like they were listening to each other.

"Well," Fidel said, "what do you think of it?"

I hesitated but moved closer. "Gy, it's so big!"

118

He laughed. "Walk around. Touch it. See how it feels."

I did and was surprised. "It feels warm, like it's living."

Fidel threw his hands apart and broke into a big wide smile. "Ah! That's good to hear."

I remembered what Mr. Wood had said. "Is it finished?"

He nodded happily, and threw me a polishing rag. "You can do that little part there, if you like. Then it is done."

He showed me the place and I polished it. The wood seemed to glow now, and the sunlight bounced off it and around it.

"Did you get it done in time?" I said.

Fidel nodded. "The work is done. Now all that remains is to deliver it." He shook his head happily, and walked around the big figures, thumping them with his big hand. "Yes, this was a hard one to do. An artist is always grateful when something turns out well."

"I'm glad it did," I said. "So I guess you can visit with us tonight. Or will you have to rush back again after dinner?"

Fidel cocked his head. "Yes, Jenny. Thank you. I get the message."

I breathed a sigh of relief. Now I wouldn't have to show him what Mr. Wood thought he ought to do.

I didn't know it at the time, but that was the

night the trouble started, and that darn Mr. Wood didn't give me the least warning about it.

13

Mom didn't work Saturday. She slept late, and after breakfast cleaned the house a little, and then went off shopping. She took all day shopping and brought back a car full of stuff that must have cost an arm and a leg. There were seven big shopping bags full, and a lot of other junk besides. Soft drinks, beer six-packs, new mops and brooms. It looked like she was really trying to spend her paycheck.

There was steak for dinner, the first we'd had in a long time. Chloris pretended she didn't recognize it. "What's this stuff?" she said.

There was salad and wine and beer and fruit dessert. It was one of the best meals we'd had in a long time. Mom didn't drop anything coming out of the kitchen. It seemed as if she wasn't as nervous and jumpy now that she had a better job and was making more money.

Chloris still wasn't talking to Fidel, at dinner or any time. She was aloof, the way she was when he first married Mom.

Just to be prepared, I had checked her reading

in Mr. Wood's forecast. It was kind of weird, and worried me. SCORPIO: *If you ask others what they expect of you instead of guessing, you can plow through whatever has to be done efficiently.*

I wondered if Daddy had some other spirit friends he could send down in case his own couldn't make it. I hadn't heard any more from her since the last time she discussed talking to his spirit. I was afraid to ask her. It was too spooky.

She could have been putting me on. And since she knew that I liked Fidel, she could have invented the whole thing on purpose to bug me.

Fidel commented on how great the meal was, and Mom thanked him. Then she asked him how he was coming along with his work, would he make his deadline and so forth. Fidel told her it was done, finished.

"Oh," Mom said. "Isn't that nice."

She didn't jump out of her chair and rush out to see it, and I felt that she should have shown some interest. I didn't know how much money Fidel made, or how much a piece of sculpture like this last one sold for. But I remembered how proud Mom was after she first met him, telling everybody of this great modern Mexican sculptor she had met.

"Yes," Fidel said. "And tonight I can relax and be with you."

Mom took another bite of steak. "Wonderful," she said.

After dinner, Chloris cleaned the table and I started doing the dishes. She was due to help dry later. I saw Fidel sit on the big chair in the living room, smoking his pipe. It's near the sofa, across from the TV set, just as it is in Kathy Kingman's house. I wondered if I should say anything, to get him over on the sofa. I wanted to but I couldn't.

Mom went into the bathroom and washed her hair. She came back, her head wrapped in a towel, and got under the dryer, near the dining room table.

It takes about an hour for her to dry her hair. I saw Fidel glance at his watch. But he didn't show any expression. He picked up the newspaper and began reading it, reloaded his pipe, and sat there alone, smoking. He doesn't watch TV as a rule, but if he had turned it on now, the sound would have been ruined by the sound of Mom's hair dryer.

She finished and put her things away, and came back. She checked with the TV schedule and turned on the set. Fidel was still sitting there smoking. Mom sat back on the sofa.

Here it comes, I told myself.

Fidel waited another moment, and then when she was settled on the sofa, he got off the big chair and came over and sat down beside Mom. Terrific, I thought.

"Don't you have any work?" Mom said.

Fidel shook his head. "All finished," he told her.

"Oh, that's right," Mom said. "So you told me."

She flipped the channel changer a few stations until she got what she wanted. "This show will probably bore you to tears," she said to Fidel.

Fidel said it didn't matter. He was just relaxing.

Mom said, "Well, if you're not interested in the show, it's really a waste of time for you to be watching. I know you would rather be doing your own work, which is probably a lot more interesting."

I could hardly bear it. I wanted to scream at her to cut it out. To shake her. Didn't she know what she was doing?

Chloris and I had finished the dishes. She went upstairs and asked if I was coming. I told her, in a little while. I went into the living room. They were just sitting, fairly close but not touching, not talking. I went over to Fidel's big chair and sat in it, and pretended I was watching the TV.

Fidel said, "How's the new job coming? Are you handling everything all right?"

"Well, of course," Mom said. "You don't think they would have picked me for the job if I was incompetent, do you?"

Fidel wagged his head. He looked gloomy.

"Actually, you're making me very uncomfortable now," Mom said. "Night after night I sit here alone while you're out there in your studio playing with your pieces of wood. You never seem to have the time to sit with me, or talk to me."

124

"I have the time now," Fidel said. "What shall we talk about?"

Mom waved her hand. "Oh, go and do your work. I don't want you acting like a martyr just to please me."

Oh, no, Mom, I pleaded silently. Don't! Don't be saying those things.

I looked at Fidel. His face was covered by a mask, so that you couldn't see any expression. But his dark eyes glittered.

Fidel, wait! I said silently. Please, wait! She didn't mean it! It's that new job she's got, and you know how nervous and jumpy she's been lately.

Fidel must have got my thought waves. He didn't get up. Other than just puffing his pipe, he didn't move. He just sat there next to her, his eyes locked on the dumb tube.

Suddenly, Mom jumped up. "Oh, this program is too stupid for words. You can watch it yourself, if you want to. I have some calls to make."

She hurried out of the room.

Dumbbell! I screamed silently. *Mom, you great big dumbbell!*

Fidel sat another moment. He ran his fingers through his thick hair. He tapped his pipe out in the bowl. Then he played with his lower lip a moment. Finally he sighed, got to his feet, walked across the room and snapped the set off. I guess he never saw me sitting there, so small in his big chair, because he walked out of the room without looking at me, without saying a word.

I heard the hammering moments later from his studio.

After a while, I dried my eyes. I had to talk to him.

Fidel didn't hear my knock at first. When he finally opened the door, he looked down at me, surprised. He didn't say anything.

"Mom didn't mean what she said, Fidel. Honest. I know her."

He rubbed his chin. "Perhaps. And then again, you may not."

"She never acts this way. Maybe she's sick or something. Anyway, I'm glad you were so good about it. That you didn't tell her off."

"No," Fidel said, shaking his head. "You are wrong there, Jenny. You don't want the argument or fight. You want a nice peaceful family and house. But to ignore her, what she was doing, was my fault."

"How do you mean?"

"It's something you will have to learn. To allow another person to do you in, is wrong. It makes you an accomplice to their destructiveness."

"I don't get it. I thought you were supposed to understand why people blow their stacks and not get mad back at them."

"It feels nice to do that, yes. You do it in the

name of your own prideful goodness. You feel you are so forgiving. But it does nothing but feed the other's feeling of power. No, Jenny—one must survive, and so it is better to learn to fight back. We are not gods to forgive others for what they do to us. If we let people step on us, they will trample us into the ground, into dust.

"Your nature, too, is to be good, to accept, not to make waves. To be a good little girl always. But it is wrong. Inside you is another part, a self that is not so nice, that wants its own voice to be heard. This is your bad side, yes, but it is part of your being, too, and must be allowed to have its say. Otherwise, you grow up putting yourself down always. That way you are never really yourself, but only part of a human being. We are all born both good and bad. We must learn to know each part of us and how to use it."

Chloris isn't so dumb, I thought. She uses all her bad.

14

Chloris had taken the sign off her door. I knocked two times anyway. I needed to know what was going on in her spirit talks, and I couldn't take a chance of offending her.

"Who is it?" she called.

Nobody ever knocks on her door but me. "It's me," I said.

"Oh, come in."

She was lying on her bed, hands clasped behind her head. "I suppose you think I didn't hear the fight," she said.

"What fight?" I said innocently. "Mom was just being bitchy. You know, like that mother on that police rookies program, who had that heart condition and she didn't want to let on."

"Mom's heart is fine," Chloris said. "She's also letting on to Fidel he can take his old Mexican sculptures and get out of our house."

"Maybe you forgot," I said. "This is *his* house. He invited us to live here with him. We only had the small apartment in Westwood."

"Big deal," she said. "So we can always move

128

back. Anyway, Mom's making more money now, so we can take a bigger place."

I remembered what Mr. Wood had said about Chloris this day. She was supposed to ask others what to do. "Have you heard anything new lately?" I said, casually. "You know, from Daddy's spirit?"

Her eyes flicked sideways to me. "Maybe," she said. "You wouldn't believe it, even if I said I had."

"Why wouldn't I? Don't forget he was my Daddy, too, even though you were his favorite."

Chloris sniffed. But I saw I had softened her up a little.

"What did he say when you told him about Mom's new job?"

Chloris smiled. "He liked that. He said that was a good start."

"For what?"

"You know, to get rid of Fidel, dumbbell. Daddy's spirit said it was time for that freaky Mexican so-called artist to find out how it felt when the woman became the breadwinner in the house."

"What does that mean?"

"It means," Chloris said patiently, "that now Mom makes more than Fidel does. That means she doesn't need him to support us. Figure it out for yourself."

I remembered the last part of what Mr. Wood

had to say about Chloris: *Instead of guessing, you can plow through whatever has to be done efficiently.*

If it was true, it meant somebody had a plan to really get rid of Fidel and break him and Mom up. It would be like lightning striking us right after hitting Kathy Kingman's house.

"Well," I said cautiously, "I don't think she'll do anything just yet, do you? I mean, she has to see how her new job works out. That she buys the right stuff and everything for Bontel's."

Chloris snickered. "Don't worry about Mom. She knows how to hold her job."

"How do you mean?" I said, nervously.

"You know," Chloris said, with heavy emphasis. "That bull all week about having to work late, and eating dinner out, and that jazz, you know what's going on, don't you?"

"You mean, where she's eating dinner? Someplace near, in Beverly Hills, I guess."

Chloris threw her arms out, shrieking with laughter. "You're really a baby, you know that? I'm not talking about where she's having dinner, but with *who* she's having dinner. You get it?"

I shook my head. "No."

"With her boss, of course. She's acting real sweet and helpless with him, batting her eyes, acting nervous and making him feel she's so grateful to him for giving her this big chance."

"How do you know that?"

"Because that's what all smart women do, to hold a job, dopey. They go out to dinner with the boss, and hold hands, and all that jazz."

"Mom wouldn't do that," I said.

"Why not?" Chloris said.

"Well, she's married, isn't she?"

Chloris laughed again and rolled over. "Gy, you're simple. Don't you ever see any movies? Sometimes they even go to the boss's apartment!"

"You mean, even if she didn't like him?"

"What's that got to do with it? She likes her new job, that's the important thing. And if the boss says, how about dropping over to my apartment for some dictation, you don't think she'll say no, do you, and lose her job, do you? Well, I don't."

"Gy," I said. "You don't know all this. You're just making it up."

Her eyes gleamed. "Wanna bet?"

"Okay, how do you know? Have you followed her around after work?"

Chloris smiled. "No, *I* haven't," she said meaningfully. "But somebody else has."

My mouth popped open. "You mean Daddy's spirit?"

"You finally guessed right," she said. "You should know spirits can go anywhere. They can walk through walls, and restaurants and nobody sees them."

"And Daddy's spirit has been following Mom?"

Chloris nodded her head up and down a few times. "And just to make sure, when he's busy and can't be around, he turns the job over to some spirit friends of his. It's like a team service, see? They all help each other any way they can."

I couldn't think of what to say. Here was one time when Mr. Wood had definitely known what was happening. His exact words were: *If you ask others what they expect of you. . .*

So he knew Daddy's spirit had other spirit friends! "Well, maybe," I said. "But I think you're wrong. I don't think Mom knows how to do dictation."

"It doesn't matter, dummy," Chloris said. "Maybe he wants her to listen to his hi-fi set. She knows how to listen, doesn't she? How can she say no to that?"

I shrugged. "I don't know."

"Well, there you are. So you see, she's getting in good with her boss so he won't fire her. And after a few more weeks, she'll know she's in solid, and then—whammo—we get rid of Fidel La Mancha!"

"What's his name?" I said.

"What's who's name?"

"Mom's boss at Bontel's."

Chloris rolled her eyes dramatically. "How should I know? Daddy's spirit didn't mention it. What's the difference?"

"What if they made a mistake? What if one of Daddy's spirit friends was just told to look for a dark-haired woman in that apartment of her boss? He doesn't know what Mom really looks like. Maybe it's somebody else who looks like Mom."

Chloris curled her lip. "Don't be ridiculous. Spirits don't make mistakes. Anyway, he would have followed her from the store to the restaurant to the apartment, wouldn't he?"

"I don't know. I suppose."

Chloris threw her hands apart expressively. "Well, then, there you are. How could the spirit have made a mistake? How many dark-haired, middle-aged women Assistant Buyers are there at Bontel's Beauty Salon Department?"

I didn't like hearing any of this junk. But I didn't want to argue with Chloris about it, because I needed to know everything that was going on, right or wrong.

"Okay," I said. "Let's suppose you're right and you got the right spirit messages. According to what you're saying, Mom gets rid of Fidel because she doesn't need his money for us to live on, right?"

"You guessed it."

"And then we move back to our old apartment or find a bigger one. Without Fidel."

Chloris waved. "You're really with it now, babe."

"Then what happens?"

Chloris narrowed her eyes. "What do you mean?"

"I mean, what you're saying, is that all this is what our Daddy's spirit wants—for Mom to get rid of Fidel?"

She bobbed her head. "Sure. That's the whole idea."

"But then she'll be alone again after divorcing Fidel. You know what that means, don't you?"

"You tell me," she said. Her voice sounded uncertain.

"So then she'll start dating different men again. Maybe her boss from Bontel's. Maybe some of the salesmen who sell her stuff. Maybe some of the other bigshots she meets on her new job. She'll start bringing them to the apartment again and you know what will happen. You won't like it and neither will Daddy's spirit. What happens if she decides to marry one of them?"

Chloris stiffened. Her eyes gleamed, her lips twisted. She picked up a small pillow from her bed and threw it at me. "Get out!" she yelled. "I hate you! Get out of here!"

She's not a very good thrower when she's mad. The pillow bounced off my knees. I picked it up and smoothed it out. It had been a present to her from Grandma Grace.

"But, it's possible, isn't it?" I said. I was still

trying to play it cool, like a Libra, not let her temper get the best of us. "Maybe Daddy's spirit didn't think of that possibility. Maybe he forgot how pretty she is."

Chloris sat now hunched over, her arms around her knees. She gave me a knowing look. "Don't you worry about Daddy's spirit. He knows, all right. He's not dumb, you know. He's got a plan!" She smiled and stretched. "Of course he knows what she'll do. But she has to get rid of Fidel first. That's Plan A! After that, we go into Plan B."

"What's Plan B?"

Chloris smirked, and wagged her head. "I'm not telling you that. It's a secret between Daddy and me. Now would you mind getting lost? I want to be alone."

I closed her door behind me. I had taken only a few steps when I heard an old familiar sound. It was Chloris crying. It made me wonder if she really had everything planned, as she said, with Daddy's spirit. But again, I couldn't be sure.

I heard another sound. The dull hammering coming from Fidel's studio. Every blow he struck on that crating he was making seemed to be taking him farther away from us.

15

I was up early Sunday morning and ran downstairs for the paper. On Sundays, there's so much junk in the newspaper, it's hard to find the astrological column with Mr. Wood's forecast. When I finally found it, I ripped it out and ran back upstairs to my room to read it.

TAURUS: *Learn to control your temper and emotions. Harsh words now will haunt you later.*

You're a day late, Mr. Wood, I told him.

Fidel's gave me some hope. MOON CHILDREN: *Plan for greater success and harmony with mate. Try to bring friends back into the fold who have strayed away.*

I nearly got an ulcer from reading the one for Chloris. SCORPIO: *You can communicate satisfactorily with others. Get your wishes known to the attention of the influential who can help you put them into effect.*

Mine was weird. LIBRA: *Improve surroundings by using your sense of color, neatness, ingenuity. Coordinate efforts with fellow workers. Entertain in p.m.*

136

I went down to make my breakfast. Bacon and eggs and toast. The bacon burned and came out charred. The egg yolks broke in the fry pan and ran together, the way I don't like them. After I buttered the toast, one slice fell off the plate, and I had to clean up the mess on the floor.

It made me wonder if Mr. Wood really knew what it was all about. So far I was way off, and the day had hardly begun. But although I had already flunked on color, neatness and ingenuity, I still had two chances left. To coordinate efforts with fellow workers. And to entertain in p.m.

I heard Fidel come inside from his studio and go upstairs. I gulped down my milk and went up quietly to my room. I left my door slightly open.

I heard Fidel, talking to Mom. "What's wrong, Margaret?"

Her voice was low, tight. "Nothing. Nothing at all."

"I thought it was understood before we married," Fidel said. "I must work whenever I can. I'm an artist, a creative person. My hours are not regular like with most people."

"Yes, I know," Mom said.

I could imagine Fidel shrugging his thick shoulders, throwing his hands apart. "Well, then. You must know my work is my motivation for living. I need the feeling that I have accomplished something original, created something."

"I know, I know," Mom said. "But dammit, you're always working. You never stop."

"I'm sorry," he said. "When I run out of creativity, it will be a sad time for me."

"That'll be the day," Mom said. "You're good for another 200 years."

Fidel waited a long time before replying. "How can I answer that?" he said finally.

"Don't bother," Mom snapped. "I get the message. You find your work more interesting than me."

Oh, Mom, I thought, worried, come on, cool it, please! I wished there was some way I could slip in there, invisible, and show her Mr. Wood's comments on how she had to button up her temper today.

"You're not talking sense," Fidel said. "Perhaps you should see a doctor. You seem too nervous lately."

"I don't need a doctor," Mom fired back.

"Perhaps it's your job. Maybe you're working too hard at it."

"It's a job," Mom said. "Just a job. I need it to support myself and my children. I told you I didn't want to interfere with your career, and make you feel you had to take care of us."

"Well, then, so what is it that's making you so nervous?"

"I don't know," Mom said. "I'm just nervous,

138

that's all. It's not just me. Look around—the whole world is nervous."

"The world will have to manage," Fidel said. "I'm concerned only about you. It's not like you to suddenly be crying for attention."

Mom broke in impatiently, her voice rising. "Oh, stop trying to analyze me. You're not a psychiatrist."

"It might not be a bad idea for you to see one," Fidel said. "If you have a problem—"

Mom interrupted. "There's nothing wrong with a woman wanting some attention. Now please leave me alone. I don't want to discuss it."

"But—"

"Go back to your work," Mom said. "That's all you're really interested in. You could have done seventeen new things while you've been up here trying to tell me something's wrong with me."

Fidel made some kind of rueful laugh. Then he walked out and went downstairs. I went to my door and heard Mom sniffling and then beginning to cry.

Chloris came out of her room. She must have had her door open like I did. She saw me and her eyes gleamed happily.

She came close to me and whispered. "What'd I tell you?"

I shook my head. "She's got a headache. That's why she's crying."

139

"I know," Chloris said. "Daddy's spirit said he was working on that."

"Huh? How do you mean?"

Chloris tapped her heart area. "He's reaching her guilty conscience."

"You're all wet," I said. "How can he do that?"

Chloris beckoned me into her room. I went reluctantly, but I had to know. "You're making all this up, Chloe."

She shook her head negative. "No I'm not. It's easy for a spirit. He's invisible, like I told you. He walks through walls. Then he just stands there near her bed, and he talks to her."

"What about?" I said nervously.

"You know what about," she said, looking angry. "About what she did to him. Now he keeps saying the same words to her, over and over again."

"What words?"

"He says, 'Why did you do it? Why did you do it? Why did you do it?' "

"Just those words?"

Chloris shrugged. "That's all he needs right now for this."

"And Mom can hear him?"

"Of course," Chloris said. "Why do you think she's breaking up?"

"How about you? Can you hear him?"

"Not when he's talking to her. He talks very softly."

140

"So how do you know what he's saying?"

Chloris looked at me with surprise. "I told you. He tells me. When he talks to me."

"I hope you're telling the truth," I said. "Otherwise, you're the freakiest one of everybody you mentioned."

Her lip curled disdainfully. "Am I? Stick around. You'll see."

I didn't want to admit it, but she had me worried now. The only good part of the morning, so far, was that Fidel did what Mr. Wood wanted him to. That "planning for harmony with mate and trying to bring friends back who have strayed away."

The doorbell downstairs chimed. "That must be Kathy," I said, and ran down. I opened the door and looked up at a tall thin boy with a lot of red hair.

"Hi," he said. "Is Chloris home?"

I nodded, surprised. I stepped back to call up the steps. "It's for you."

She came to the landing and leaned over the rail. "Who is it?"

I turned back to the boy at the door. "Who's calling please?" I said.

"Rick Harrison," he said.

I stepped back again and yelled up. "Rick Harrison."

She came running down so fast I thought she

would break a leg. Then she stopped suddenly and began to walk the rest of the way to the door very casually and slowly. As if she didn't care who was waiting out there.

As she passed me, I whispered, "You're right. He does look kind of freaky."

She ignored me and walked past, her head high. She pulled the door behind her as she went out, but I heard her voice, warm and excited. "Hi, Rick. What are you doing up this way?"

I couldn't hear his answer. But from the sweet and gushy way Chloris spoke to him, I knew what she had told me before about him being a freak, was strictly for the birds. He was only a freak then, it seemed, because he went for Alice Packer instead. Being a freak depended a lot upon whether Chloris was jealous of somebody. I could hardly wait now for her to come home and rave about how terrific this Rick Harrison was.

That was okay with me. I figured if Chloris got to like somebody and got liked in return, then maybe she would lose some of her rotten disposition, and things might be better around the house.

I heard somewhere that love could work miracles.

16

Mom came downstairs later and made breakfast. She looked pale and her eyes were puffy and red-rimmed.

"Where's your sister?" she said.

"Outside."

Mom nodded and took another sip of her coffee. "When she comes in," she said, "tell her I made an appointment for her with Dr. Smythe tomorrow after school."

Dr. Smythe was the lady shrink therapist in Beverly Hills Chloris had spent a lot of time with a few years ago. When she was very hung-up on our dead Daddy, and wouldn't admit that Fidel was Mom's new husband.

Chloris used to come back crying, telling me that all these shrinks wanted was to mess you up so that you couldn't believe in your own thinking any more. "Dr. Smythe is a real creep," she said then. "She wants me to try to forget Daddy. Can you imagine a creepy finky shrink like that?"

I told her I couldn't.

"She thinks I'm overdoing it a bit," Chloris said.

"That I have to accept the fact Daddy is dead and go on with my own life. Can you imagine having to pay $30 every week for that kind of dumb advice?"

"That's a lot," I said. "How can Mom afford it?"

"I don't care about that," Chloris said. "It was her own dumb idea in the first place. She's doing it so I can like Fidel. There's no way I'll ever like that fat creep."

She stayed sullen and silent against him for a long time, ignoring Fidel as if he was invisible. Fidel kept his cool and didn't let on he noticed. Then, after a year, suddenly somehow Chloris changed. She became friendlier, and said hello to him, and generally acted as if she knew he was alive.

Now, it was two years later, and she was starting the same dopey Daddy's-girl bit all over again. Only worse, it seemed to me, this time. All that stuff about her talking with Daddy's spirit scared me.

I looked at Mom now, wondering how much she really knew about Chloris. There wasn't a lot I could say though, because she was still my sister.

"Okay, I'll tell her," I said. "Only I don't think she'll be crazy about the idea. Chloris didn't go very much for Dr. Smythe, you know."

"That's too bad," Mom said. "In case I don't

144

have a chance to talk to her, tell her I want her ready right after school. I'll pick her up at 3:00."

"You're coming back all the way here to take her there?"

"Well, of course," Mom said. "How else would she get there?"

"She could take a taxi."

Mom looked at me as if I'd just stepped on her foot. "Taxis are expensive. I'll pick her up."

"But how can you get off from your job?"

"Don't worry," Mom said calmly. "They understand a person needs to see a doctor sometimes."

Mom did her dishes after she finished her coffee and went back upstairs. I didn't know what to do. I felt like going outside but I didn't want Chloris thinking I might be spying on her and Rick Harrison. I thought of calling Kathy but decided against it. It was still early in the day and there was still a lot of time left for us to get together. There wasn't much else to do, so finally I went back upstairs and got out my books and began my book report on George Washington.

I wasn't very far into it when I heard the downstairs door close. Chloris came up the stairs humming softly. She went directly to her room, ignoring my open door invitation. I figured it was a good time to give her Mom's message and find out how things were between her and Rick, at the same time.

Her door was closed and I could hear her radio playing. It sounded like the Jefferson Starship group. I knocked twice and opened the door before she had a chance to think about it.

She was lying on her bed, one leg crossed on her knee, keeping time with the music. "Oh, it's you," she said. "I had an idea you'd be around to bug me."

"I got a message—" I began.

Chloris cut me off, smiling. "Alice Packer, I guess, huh? Well, she's out of luck. Rick told me he wasn't going to see her any more."

"How come?" I went over and turned her radio low.

"Because he likes *me*. That's how come."

"I mean, how do you know, for sure?"

Chloris pushed back her hair and sat up, hugging her knees. "Oh, you get to know these things," she said with a secretive smile. "Boys are pretty easy to figure out, you know."

"Yeah, I suppose," I said. "But won't Alice be mad at you now? I mean, for taking Rick away from her?"

Chloris shrugged. "Who cares? I mean, I didn't drag him here, did I? He came to see me of his own free will, didn't he?"

"I guess so. I don't know. What did you do— take a walk with him?"

"Something like that," Chloris said. "He wanted to show me his new bike. It's a 10-speed Mirage.

146

That's French, you know. Real neat. Sort of yellow."

"Well, how come you came back so soon?" I said. "Did you have a fight?"

"Of course not. Rick didn't have much time today, so he just drove up to see me, he said, and kind of get things straight. About him and Alice, I mean. I knew she would be kind of worried and call."

"You did?"

Chloris nodded smugly. "She thought she had him all to herself. What exactly did she tell you on the phone? Did she ask if Rick was here?"

"Uh-uh," I said, wagging my head. "In fact, she didn't even call."

Chloris froze. Her eyes gleamed, "I thought you told me you had a message for me."

"Yeah, but that was from Mom, not Alice."

Chloris sighed and made her voice dramatic. "Oh, and what did *she* want?"

"She said to tell you to wait here after school tomorrow. You got a new appointment with Dr. Smythe."

Chloris swung her legs off the bed, yelling, "What? That creepy finky shrink again? Nothing doing! I'm not starting up with her again!"

I shrugged. I didn't expect her to be happy about it. "Anyway, that's what Mom said to tell you, in case she didn't get the chance."

Chloris jerked her thumb to the door. "Okay,

you told me. Now get lost. But if she thinks I'm going, she has another think coming. She's trying to get out of it and make believe I'm the one who's sick. It's all her fault. She's the one who made our Daddy kill himself!"

The door opened and I jumped back a foot. Mom was standing there. Her eyes were blazing mad, her face paler than I ever saw it. She took a step toward Chloris. "What was that you just said?"

Chloris only stared, unable to speak. She licked her lips. Mom took a deep breath. "I'm asking you again—what did you say?"

Chloris stood mutely shaking her head. I could see tiny beads of perspiration on her forehead.

Mom was so mad, her voice was harsh, low and growling, in a way I'd never heard before. Her fists clenched and unclenched. "I heard what you said. Your door was open, so I couldn't help but hear you. Is that what you really think—that it was my fault your father killed himself? Well, answer me!"

Chloris stood there still not saying a word. Her eyes were hard, like Mom's, and they stood there glaring at each other. It was my fault for not closing the door when I came in, but so far Chloris wasn't blaming me. She had all her attention fixed on Mom.

Mom turned to me. "Is that what you believe too, Jenny? What your sister thinks?"

It was the first time the question ever came up so that I had to think about it. "Well, no, not exactly. I mean, well—I don't know. But I don't think so. I mean—"

It was the Libra in me, trying to get it all balanced and not doing it very well. I felt my face growing red.

Mom stepped back, her face looking strained and tired. "That's fine," she said, not hiding her disappointment. "Just fine. Instead of two loving daughters, I have—" She shook her head and pushed back her hair. "I don't know what I have."

She turned and walked out of the room. I ran after her. "Chloris didn't mean what she said," I told her. "She just—well, she gets excited some-times . . . you know?"

Mom looked at me with an annoyed expression. "And what about you? Were you excited, too?" She waited for me to answer. I couldn't think of an excuse. Mom curled her lip. "That's what I thought. Well, I can see we have to get certain things straight around here." She glanced at her watch. "I want both you and your sister downstairs in exactly ten minutes. And then I want you to ask Fidel if he can spare the time to join us in the dining room."

"What is it?" I said. "A family meeting?"

Mom nodded, her face sullen and hard. "You might call it that."

She headed back into her room and closed the

door. I heard her on the phone, asking to talk to Dr. Smythe. Chloris stuck her head out the door to listen. She didn't see me.

I was tired of eavesdropping, hearing all these things that made my stomach churn. I went downstairs to give Fidel Mom's message. He didn't ask any questions. He said okay, he would be right in. I felt like Paul Revere, going around, knocking on doors, telling people something was up, they better get ready. I wondered if anybody on the way told him not to bother them, to get lost.

It wasn't for my country, but I bet I was as nervous as Paul was.

17

Mom sat Chloris and me around the dining room table. She caught Fidel's questioning expression. "You can sit, too, if you like, Fidel. There's a little problem I have with my girls regarding my previous marriage. It needs clearing up. And I'd like you here in case you might have some questions, too. You've had some before, and perhaps now you'll be satisfied with my answers."

Fidel tapped his pipe. "Will it be all right to smoke? This seems like such a serious meeting."

I smiled but Mom didn't. At another time, she would have laughed. I think I can tell now when something is wrong. It's when people lose their sense of humor. They get all wrapped up in what they're thinking, and can't see past that. I had the feeling that even the argument between Kathy's mother and father might have blown over, if either one of them would have not taken it so seriously, and laughed about it, instead.

"Girls," Mom said, "we're going to discuss my divorce from your father. I don't think that really concerns you, but because of his suicide later, after

151

his next marriage, it might be better for you to know the whole story. Then perhaps you'll understand what really happened."

Chloris looked bored. She kept playing with a rubber band around her wrist. "Stop that," Mom said. Chloris stopped. She started to tap her fingers on the table. Mom looked at her steadily for a moment, but didn't say anything. Chloris kept drumming her fingers as if she were playing a tune.

Mom sat down at one end of the long dining room table. Fidel sat at the other side, and got his pipe going. Chloris and I sat opposite each other, me on Mom's right, Chloe on her left. The smoke from Fidel's pipe formed like a blue cloud over his head, drifting very slowly until it fell apart.

Mom began talking, her voice low and serious. "Your father and I met in college. We fell in love after dating a few times. After college, we decided to get married. He had studied to be an attorney, then he added courses to it to become a patent attorney.

"He wasn't making much money when we got married. I had to get a job in a department store. My parents loaned us money. They bought us our first house and also the furniture, every single piece in it. From time to time, when we couldn't pay our bills, they helped us with more money.

"Finally your father got the hang of what he was doing. He learned how to make money. He got so good at it, he started working later and later at his office, to make more money. I was home alone evenings. I was lonely. I didn't know what to do with myself. But he explained we needed security and I had to admit we did. Then after a few years, I became pregnant."

I grinned at Chloris. "Hear that? You're almost born."

She sniffed. "Big deal."

Mom went on. "What I didn't know then, was how your father's mother, Grandma Helen, had brought him up. She was very firm with him, kept him tied to her apron strings. She made him into a mama's boy. He couldn't make any decision of his own, he always had to ask her about it. Even when he was a grown man, he still didn't trust his own judgment, he had to talk things over with her."

"What about Grandpa?" I said. "Didn't he say something?"

"Not enough, I'm afraid," Mom said. "He was afraid of her, too."

"Gy!"

"Then when I became pregnant with Chloris, Larry—your father—became frightened. He was afraid of the responsibility of being a father. He acted as if he didn't love me any more. We had some arguments about it and he left."

I looked at Chloris to make sure she got this. She didn't blink an eye. She looked bored.

"The night I went to the hospital for my first baby, he wasn't around," Mom said, tears brimming in her eyes. "Then afterward he came around, tried to make things over. I didn't want to bring up my child without her father. So we got back together. Everything went pretty much as it did before. He kept working very hard, even weekends at his office. I still wasn't happy about that. Then I became pregnant with Jenny."

It was my turn to feel embarrassed. I wondered what I had looked like as a baby. I remember Grandma Grace always kept telling me what a cute fat baby I was. You'd never know it now. All that baby fat is really gone.

Mom sighed. "The few years together made no difference. Your father was upset again at the idea of now having two children—more responsibility. He started avoiding me again, hardly ever seeing me, or talking to me. When Jenny was born, he had already moved out."

Chloris looked stonily at me.

"This time I was really angry. I started action for a divorce. But he talked me out of it. He said he still loved me. I thought I still loved him, too, and shouldn't blame him for being weak when I wanted him to be strong and dependable.

"But it didn't last. We had more arguments than ever. We hardly ever spoke when he was home. I told him it was all over. He seemed to agree.

He said he didn't want his life tied up with kids, having to be a father. So we got divorced.

"He was awarded visiting rights. He saw you girls on Wednesday nights and Saturday mornings. Sometimes he would call at the last minute, say he was busy and couldn't make it. Eventually it became just Saturday morning visits. He used to take you down to his office while he finished some work, or out to his boat. Then he married his secretary. You knew her. Cindy. I didn't know he intended getting married that soon after our divorce."

Chloris stared at her fingers. She started to entwine them from different hand positions. Fidel continued smoking. I remembered some parts of what Mom was telling. The boat and eating out at taco drive-in places. Cleaning the boat for a quarter apiece, and nothing if we didn't do it right. Good times singing in his car. Bad times when me or Chloris happened to be crying about something. I couldn't remember what.
"Then Cindy, his new wife, became pregnant," Mom said. "And before her child was born, he left her. Just as he had left me. He went to live alone on his boat. And shortly after that, I was notified that he had shot and killed himself."

She looked at Fidel and then back at us. "Nobody ever knew why. He didn't leave a suicide note. His business was not as good as it had been, but it wasn't bad. He had bought a lot of property, made a lot of investments. Some had failed but he wasn't broke, or desperate enough to kill himself for that reason.

"That's all I know. That's the whole story. I told you girls some of it years ago, when it happened. You were both too young to remember. Now I'm telling it to you hoping you will understand everything there is to know about it. And then, I'd like to forget it. It's not good constantly raking over the past. A doctor told me that once, when I needed his help, and it's true. So now that you both know, I hope we can put it to rest, and forget."

I was about to push my chair away and get off my seat. Chloris said, "You forgot something."

Mom flushed. "What did I forget?"

"You left out something. You left out two things."

"What two things? What did I leave out?"

"You left out that my Daddy still loved you. He didn't want to be divorced."

Mom frowned. "How would you know?"

"He told me after it happened. On his boat. I remember."

Mom's fingers tapped the table. "Well, maybe he did love me, or thought he did. But he had deserted me twice at the most important times of my life. I didn't want to be with him any more.

I wanted a new life, so I divorced him. If two people don't feel the same way about each other, if they don't love each other, there's no reason to stay married."

Chloris shrugged her shoulders. "Maybe. Only he said you loved him, too. That you were divorcing him for spite, to teach him a lesson."

"Oh, for goodness sakes!" Mom said. "That's ridiculous! We hadn't loved each other for weeks, for months! If there was any love left, it was all in his imagination. You know, some people can't bear to give up something they thought they owned, even if they don't want it any longer."

"So how come you tried to get him arrested, put in jail?" Chloris said. "I know about that, too."

Mom tossed her hair back angrily. "What? I never did that! Is that some other silly lie he put into your head?"

I leaned forward to hear what Chloris had to say. Fidel seemed intent on her answer, too. He was frowning, his dark eyes locked on my sister.

"He told me," Chloris said with a stubborn expression. "He showed me the letter from your lawyer. The retrain junction to put him in jail!"

Mom blinked, looking bewildered. Then she smiled. "Oh, you mean the restraint injunction? Well, yes, I had to ask my lawyer to do that."

"*Como?*" Fidel said, folding his thick arms. "What's that about?"

Mom shook her head, looking annoyed. "It's something I was advised to do. Larry was upset over my divorcing him. He would call me, at all hours of the night. Pleading. Writing me letters. Threatening about what he might do if he saw me with another man.

"I consulted my lawyer and he drew up the paper with my complaint. It wasn't anything about throwing Larry in jail!"

"It was, too!" Chloris shouted. "Daddy showed me the paper! He read it to me. I remember."

Mom bit her lips, her eyes wide and angry. "The paper was a common legal form to restrain him. It was signed by a judge. It said he was not to bother me. He had to promise and agree not to call or talk to me, to see me at my home, to threaten or follow me. He knew the law; he had studied it. So he signed the agreement. I had my own life to lead with you girls, to bring you up as I thought best. I didn't want him interfering any longer."

Chloris raised her voice and spoke faster. "That's why he killed himself. Because you wouldn't listen. Because you were going to arrest him and throw him in jail if he tried to talk to you or write to you that he loved you. That's why he killed himself. It didn't have anything to do with Cindy, his new wife, or her baby."

Mom's hand was at her throat. She looked

158

shocked. "Now don't tell me you know that, too. Did he tell you that before he killed himself? Now, if that's what you want to believe, then go on, believe it. It's not the truth but I can't seem to get it right inside your head.

"Don't forget, it was three years later that your father did what he did. If he wanted to kill himself over the court order, he would have done it a lot sooner."

"I know why he did it," Chloris said sullenly. "He did it to show you. Because you wouldn't listen. Because he couldn't talk to you."

Mom looked across the table at Fidel. "What is she talking about?"

Fidel frowned and tapped his pipe out. "It is only her guess but it is something to think about."

"What? For God's sake, what?" Mom yelled.

"It was the piece of paper, perhaps?" Fidel said. "If he could not talk to you or get you to listen, he was frustrated. A man who will kill himself has lost his esteem. His own self. So perhaps then your husband had one way left for his message. If you would not notice him again alive, he knew a way. When he killed himself, he knew you would have to notice him, to pay attention."

Mom pushed herself away from the table. She stood up, her face drawn and pale. Her hand came up and pushed back her long dark hair. She stared at Fidel. The tip of her tongue licked at her lips.

Her voice was hoarse. "Are you saying then, that it was my fault? That he killed himself over me, because I divorced him?"

I felt awfully hot and embarrassed. I hoped Fidel would say something nice to calm her down.

He shook his head. "No, Margaret. Never would I say that, or think it. It was a possibility. He left no note. There are many other possibilities. Perhaps the truth will never be known."

Mom began to tremble. "But meanwhile I'm suspect, is that it? Because I had to divorce a man I could no longer trust to be the man I wanted? Even if he had threatened to kill himself if I divorced him, is my own life to be stopped by that kind of blackmail? What about my own right to live? To bring up my children the way I want to? Am I to give that up because a man says he loves me, is too weak to stand on his own feet as a man?"

Fidel spoke slowly and calmly. "No one is judging you. The matter had to be examined again before the children. You did what you had to do. When your girls grow up, they may have a similar problem. It is not easy to face up to what you want for yourself, when another would try to stop you. To make it seem as if his life is in your hands if you go your own way. I agree. Yes, that is blackmail."

Mom's voice broke. "Then, are you satisfied?

Are you all satisfied? The trial is over. Am I guilty?"

Chloris didn't say anything. She kept staring at her hands locked in front of her on the table. I wanted to say something but I didn't know what to say.

Mom took a deep breath then, and suddenly broke away from the table. She was crying when she ran up the stairs. I heard the door slam in her room.

Fidel stood up. He looked at Chloris. There wasn't any mistake that he was talking to her.

"You owe your mother an apology, I think. Your father has twisted your thinking somehow, and it is very sad. You are not a district attorney, but instead a very mixed-up little girl. But you are old enough now to have your own responsibility to others. You cannot hurt and destroy people out of your own ignorance and malice.

"We bury the dead. We pray over their graves and we weep for those we love who have gone from our hearts. But then we go on with the business of living our own lives. We must not cling or hold on to skeletons of the past. The past is past. Forget it, Chloris, or you will destroy your own life too. Do you understand?"

Chloris looked at him. She stared at him and tried to give him the gleaming eye treatment. Fidel's eyes held, intense, unblinking.

Chloris's lip began to tremble.

"Oh, leave me alone," she cried, and ran upstairs to her room.

Fidel and I were the only ones left at the meeting.

"What do you think, Jennifer? What's your opinion."

"Gy," I said. "I don't know. I was too young then. I hardly remember him."

"Yes," he said. "But now what do you think?"

"Well, first, I think it's so dumb! I mean, if he loved Mom so much that he couldn't stand it, I feel sorry for him. But if he took his life for that reason, what good did that do? That didn't bring her back to him.

"And anyway, it doesn't matter what reason he did have. Here his new little child was almost ready to be born, and he didn't care to wait and see it. Like he didn't even care. And he didn't think or care about Chloris and me when he did it, about who would take care of us, or how we would grow up.

"So all he thought and felt about was himself. So why should I worry about it?"

Fidel nodded. "You know, Jenny," he said, "I couldn't agree with you more."

"The only thing I don't like, is how you can divorce somebody who still loves you. Okay, so he made a few mistakes. When you get married,

162

don't they say something like 'for better or worse, and till Death do you part?' Maybe Mom forgot all about that. She got to thinking about her hurt feelings, and she forgot all about what she promised when she got married."

"Yes," Fidel said, "but then if everybody remembered their marriage vows, there would be no divorces."

"That's okay with me," I said.

18

Fidel left early Monday morning for San Francisco. He had to get there as soon as he could, to arrange his exhibits for the art gallery. A truck came along with two big guys. Fidel helped, and they really sweated getting those big constructions out of his studio. One was so big, they had to remove the door to get it through.

He didn't say anything about the family meeting we had. He just rumpled my hair and kissed me on the forehead, as usual.

"When are you coming back?" I said.

He shrugged. "Maybe Friday. It will take several days to put everything in its place. This is an important show for me, and everything must be placed in the gallery's best light."

I wished him luck. He smiled happily, hugged me, told me to take care of myself, and so on.

Mom had already left for Bontel's, even earlier than usual, to beat the Monday morning freeway jams. After Fidel left, I made my breakfast. Chloris had a later bus than I did, and I checked Mr. Wood's astrological forecast: TAURUS (Mom's):

164

Calm down a partner and reach a good under-standing for mutual benefit. Avoid trouble!

You're a day late again, Woodsie, I thought.

Fidel's seemed okay for his trip. MOON CHIL-DREN: *Gain the support of bigwigs for your highest aims. Go after your collections and then pay bills. Command higher salary.*

Make a lot of money, Fidel, I breathed silently. Then maybe Mom won't be making such a big deal about her new job to put you down.

I didn't like the one for Chloris. SCORPIO: *Plan early for a new way of life and then get the wheels rolling in the right direction. Secure aid and advice from influential persons.*

Mine was terrific, the best one Mr. Wood had given me so far. LIBRA: *Improve your plans so you turn chaos into greater success. Contact as many key persons as you can. Show you are definitely on the ball.*

It was just what I wanted. But that part about contacting key persons bugged me. I didn't know any key persons.

I also didn't know how I was going to turn chaos into success, but if Mr. Wood thought I could, I wasn't going to let him down. If I did, it probably would have been the last time he gave me a chance to help in the family crisis.

I looked up Kathy's. CAPRICORN: *Make certain you know what you want to achieve now, then use the right methods to gain your aims. Discuss with associates how to advance.*

Kathy's was even better than mine. She had me for an associate. I still needed a key person.

I called her on the phone and read it off. "You can discuss your methods with me, if you like, Kathy."

"Okay. I want them to get back together here. How am I going to do that?"

"I don't know," I said. "It's supposed to be your own method."

"Well, I don't have the method. All I have is the wish. Is that the same thing?"

"I don't think so. I'll meet you outside for the bus and maybe by then you'll have the method."

Chloris came downstairs. She looked half-asleep. Her hair wasn't brushed out yet. She picked up the paper, yawning. "Where's everybody?"

"Mom left for work. Fidel's moved his stuff to a gallery in San Francisco for his new show. Isn't that terrific?"

"I'll say," she said, without expression. She turned the paper over and I saw her glance at the astrological forecast. I still hadn't had time to cut it out. I never knew Chloris to read them, but she did this time. She threw the paper back on the chair.

"Neat-o," she said.

"What is?" I said.

166

She yawned and pattered away. "Seems like things are going to be okay around here, after all."

I stared at her. Apparently the whole family meeting was a waste, so far as she was concerned. I wondered if maybe, during the night, she and Daddy's spirit had made contact. Chloris looked much too confident to suit me. But I didn't want to ask and have my whole new day spoiled right at the start.

I got out fast and met Kathy at the bus stop. She looked depressed but didn't say anything about the home front. I didn't discuss ours, either.

Nobody bothered us on the bus. That was kind of depressing, too. Like nobody knew we were alive.

Mr. Farrell looked swell. He had a neat clean sport shirt on, and wore a different sport coat. He had a clean shave, his hair was brushed, and his eyes weren't red.

"What happened?" Kathy said. "Did your wife make up with you?"

He grinned. "Better than that. I got hauled into the tank for drunk driving."

"Well, anyway, you look better," I said.

He nodded. "It sobered me up. I went home, took a shower, and put on some clean clothes. Then I got the best news of all."

Kathy and I joined in. "What was that, Mr. Farrell?"

"A note from my wife that she was leaving me."

"But I thought that's what you didn't want," I said.

"That's what I thought before," Mr. Farrell said. "But this time, when I thought about it, I was sober."

Kathy asked if he had another girl friend lined up.

"I know some teachers here. They're all pretty tough, though. I think I'd rather have a Go-Go girl. You don't have to buy them a lot of clothes."

Then Mr. Farrell called the class to order and really made us sweat. I was getting to like Mr. Farrell better the other way, when he acted kind of potted, waved his hands, and acted like he didn't care.

Mr. Heartland's English class was a pain, too. He wanted us to write an essay. Nobody knew what that meant. Anything you care to write about, he said. Maybe something that happened to you lately, some incident. Or it could be about some person you met and liked. Or an animal.

I didn't know any animals, and I hadn't met anybody I knew lately that I liked. That left the family meeting, which was an incident, I thought, only I didn't feel like writing about it. Finally I made up something about the mama deer I see sometimes up in the hills over our house, and what she might be telling her babies. About looking out

168

for rattlesnakes, or people with guns, or that canyon traffic, and so on.

Mr. Heartland looked up from the book he was reading to ask us how we were doing on our book reports. We all said "Great." He nodded, and kept on reading.

The bus ride home wasn't much better than the morning one. All the kids were quiet and sat staring out the window, or at their shoes, like they all had problems. It only got a little more exciting at the bus stops, when some of the kids getting off began pushing each other back and forth. Kathy and I were about the last ones off up the canyon, and there was nobody left to push us.

The telephone was ringing when I opened our door. I picked it up and some woman asked if Mr. Carpenter was there. I said there wasn't any Mr. Carpenter.

"Gene Carpenter?" she said.

"No. But my name is Jenny Carpenter."

"That must be it," she said. "I'm calling for Mr. Wood. Mr. Wilson Wood. Are you the party who asked for some information about a Taurus native?"

"Yeah," I said excitedly. "You mean you got it already?"

"Oh, dear, no," she said frostily. "I'm Mr. Wood's secretary. He can't really do anything about your request without having the precise information. That is, the exact time of birth, year, place of birth, and so on. You left that out, Mr. Carpenter."

"Will you hold on a second," I said, "I can get it for you."

"Well—" she said uncertainly, but I was already flying up the stairs.

I found the box in Mom's bureau drawer where she keeps her personals, her marriage and birth certificates. I ran down again full speed hoping the secretary hadn't hung up.

"May 13, 1933. 5:35 a.m. Detroit, Michigan," I said. "Hello, you still there?"

"Thank you. I'll give the information to Mr. Wood. You may be hearing from him soon. You must realize that he gets hundreds of requests daily."

"I know," I said. "But this one is important."

"That's what they all say," the secretary said.

I was about to ask if there was going to be any charge, but she hung up. I was really thrilled. I never expected Mr. Wood would answer my letter. It was so great having his secretary call me, that I didn't even mind how dumb she was, not catching on that I was a girl, and still calling me Mr. Carpenter.

I replaced Mom's birth certificate in her file box, next to her two marriage certificates. She was due home soon to pick up Chloris, and I didn't

170

want to be caught snooping. I had an excuse considering it was all for the good of the family, but I didn't think Mom would go along with that.

I was doing my homework when Chloris came home. She went to her room without saying anything, and closed her door. She gets moody that way sometimes.

A horn beeped outside. Three times. I couldn't see out the front from my window, but it was 3:00, and it had to be Mom.

I rapped on Chloris's door. "Mom's honking. Remember, you got that appointment with Dr. Smythe."

"Oh, who cares," Chloris answered.

The front door opened. Mom came in looking mad. She saw me coming down the steps. "Where's your sister?" Then she saw Chloris walking down dragging one foot after the other. Mom glared and told her to hurry it up.

Chloris looked annoyed. "She didn't do me any good last time. What makes you think she got smarter now?"

Mom didn't bother answering, and stalked out. Chloris looked at me, sighed and shrugged as if helpless, and followed. Mom didn't waste any time waiting for Chloris to get settled and comfortable. She shot her old Mustang out of the driveway and headed down the canyon as if she forgot all about that 25-an-hour speed limit.

A little later, the phone rang again. I thought it might be Kathy, but I was wrong. It was a strange voice. A man.

Mr. Wood? I wondered nervously.

"Hello, is your mother home yet?"

I had heard about these callers who want to know if your mother is home or not, so they can come over and rob you. "Who's calling?" I said.

"Duane Turner."

"She's not home."

"Tell her I called, please."

"Okay. What's your number?"

"She has it," he said and hung up.

As I was getting away, the phone rang again. This time it was Kathy. "What's new over your place?" she said.

"I'm not sure," I said. "Some guy just called and asked for my mother."

"That's nothing," Kathy said. "My mother's way ahead. She's got a date with this new guy already. Tonight."

"Gy!" I said.

"That's the way I feel," Kathy said.

Chloris and Mom came home about 5:00. Chloris was holding a big box under her arm. Mom looked very upset and tired. It could have been the traffic, and then again it could have been Chloris. She can wear a person out just as fast.

I followed her upstairs. "How did it go?"

She walked into her room sullenly. "How do you think?"

"What's in the box?"

Chloris put it down on her desk. "Oh, something I got to do to make my shrink doctor happy."

She opened it up and I was puzzled. "A tape recorder? What's it for?"

Chloris frowned. "I finally got tired of Dr. Smythe saying it was time I shaped up and began to face reality. I told her I was doing only what my Daddy told me to. She wanted to know about that. So I told her about the agreement Daddy and I made, and about his spirit coming to talk to me."

"Gy, and what did Dr. Smythe say?"

"She said no spirit was talking. It was all my imagination."

"And what did you say?"

"I told her it wasn't. That I could hear my Daddy's spirit talking to me as clearly as I could hear her."

"So what did she say to that?"

Chloris tapped the tape recorder. "She gave me this to put on when I go to sleep. She said to keep it running all night. She wants to hear what Daddy's spirit has to say."

19

I left Chloris and got back to George Washington. He was having a tough time at Valley Forge. A lot of the soldiers were saying, "Who needs this?" and shoving off. The picture in the book showed him crossing the Delaware in a rowboat, in the middle of winter, just himself and a few crewmen. It looked as if that was all of the army left to fight the British. I felt sorry for him then, all alone, and then remembered the message I had to give Mom.

I ran down. She was sitting on the sofa looking pooped. "You got a phone call," I told her. "A Mr. Duane. No, a Duane Turner."

Mom looked pleased. "Did he leave a message?"

"Uh-uh. He said you knew his number."

"Oh," Mom said, pushing back her hair. "Thank you, Jenny." She got up heading for the phone in the living room.

"Who's he?" I said.

"Oh, just a friend," Mom said. There was some color in her cheeks now, and her eyes were happy. She saw me standing there. "Don't you have any homework?" I nodded and started for the steps. Mom picked up the phone. She began dialing, humming a tune softly.

I heard her from the top of the steps. "Hello, Duane? Yes, I just got the message you called ... that was Jenny, my youngest." Then he must have said something funny because she laughed. She began talking again, then stopped and laughed, then got talking again. She sounded happy, animated, lively.

I didn't want to listen and went into my room, closing my door. I got back to George Washington. He was trying to get some money to give his soldiers their back pay. Nobody wanted to shell out money. They acted like it was his war, and if he wanted to fight it, he could do it by himself. There wasn't any food for his men, and a lot more took off. At this point, it looked as if George would be lucky to get out of his war alive, let alone ever becoming Father of his country.

I got depressed and closed the book. Chloris had her door closed. Maybe she was talking to Daddy's spirit or one of his buddy spirits. I hoped the tape machine was getting everything down. This was the day when she had to plan early for a new way of life and then get the wheels rolling in the right direction. Mr. Wood sure guessed right about those tape recorder wheels.

I still had to improve my own plans, according

to the horoscope, to turn all the chaos into greater success. But I didn't have any plans. I had to hope the chaos would go away by itself and leave me alone.

I also had to contact key persons and get on the ball. I didn't know any more key persons than I did bigwigs. Mr. Wood was driving me up the wall. I hoped he would answer my letter soon.

Mom was off the phone when I got downstairs. I heard things banging around in the kitchen. She was taking stuff out of the refrigerator.

"What's your sister doing?"

I shrugged. "Her homework, maybe. Or taking a nap." I didn't want to get into the spirit talk with Mom.

"Wake her up, please, and tell her to come down. We're having dinner early."

"How come?"

"Because I'm having company. That's how come."

"That Mr. Turner?"

Mom was busy over the sink. She pushed her hair back. "That's right. Now will you please get your sister."

I started away and then stopped. "What's for dinner?"

She turned and gave me an annoyed look. "You'll know when you sit down at the table. Why are you asking so many questions?"

"I don't know," I mumbled.

176

Mom nodded as if she didn't really care what I said. She began taking stuff out of the freezer, pulling things out of the pantry room, moving fast.

Today was her day to calm down a partner and reach a good understanding for mutual benefit. To avoid trouble!

Mr. Wood may have guessed right about Chloris and her tape machine. But there was nothing in his forecast about this Mr. Turner. I didn't think he was any way to avoid trouble, at all. Just the opposite, I thought, worried.

I gave Chloris three hard knocks on the door and she still wasn't happy. I told her what Mom said about coming down for dinner. I noticed her tape recorder box was closed.

"What's the big rush?"

"I don't know. She wants to get it over with early, she said. Anyway, she's having company over."

Chloris made her eyes look doubtful. "Oh, yeah? Who?"

"I don't know. Some Mr. Turner. Duane Turner."

She screwed up her nose. "Who's he?"

"I don't know. A friend, she said."

"She's not wasting any time, is she?" Chloris said.

I didn't say anything. This was one of the few times I happened to agree with her.

Dinner was hamburgers and instant rice, sliced

tomatoes and carrots. Mom served it up fast and ate hers in a hurry. She finished first and got up from the table. "I'm going to have a bath and get dressed. When you girls are finished, make sure you clean up and put everything away."

"Who's coming over?" Chloris said.

"A friend," Mom said. She was out of the room and humming all the way up the stairs.

Chloris cocked her head. "What's with her tonight."

I said my usual. "I don't know."

"Anyway she's happy for a change. I wonder what he looks like?"

"Who?"

Chloris ignored me. "Boy, she sure makes crummy hamburgers." She put down the half-eaten bun and burger.

"Mine's okay," I said. "It just needs ketchup."

"Oh, you, you like everything."

Chloris dumped half her plate down the drain. We did the dishes and put things away. Chloris finished first and began dancing around the kitchen, humming, trying to look graceful. I got so nervous watching her, I dropped a spoon down the garbage disposal in the sink. Luckily, the switch was off.

Chloris heard me yelp and rushed over. "What did you drop?" I told her. "Don't touch anything." She stuck her hand in, reached down, and came up with it. "There you are."

I was so surprised I forgot to thank her.

We put out the light and Chloris danced all the way upstairs. We could hear Mom humming in the bathroom.

"I bet he's good-looking," Chloris said.

I didn't ask who this time. I knew.

She went into her room but didn't close the door. She kept dancing, smiling, a dreamy look on her face. I felt like socking her.

"Have you heard anything lately?" I said. I jabbed my thumb upward. "You know, from the spirit world."

"Maybe," she said. "But I can't tell you. That stuff is all confidential, you know."

"Maybe you can give me a hint," I said. "I'll figure out the rest. Okay?"

She thought about it for a second. "It's Plan A," she said. "The final phase, I think."

"Gy, what does that mean?"

"You said you'd figure it out, remember?"

While Mom was getting dressed, Chloris called one of her friends, Debbie. The upstairs phone has a long cord which can reach into any one of our rooms. She took the phone into her room. I heard her talking about Alice Packer. She was giggling, having a good time blasting Alice.

I put on the TV in my room but couldn't keep my mind on what anybody was saying. My stomach felt funny. I wondered if Chloris was right about Mom's hamburgers.

After a while, Chloris finished talking and came out to replace the phone. Mom came out of her room. She was all dressed, wearing her dark blue dress, her hair nice and shining, her eyes made up. She looked like she was going out on a date.

Chloris whistled. Mom smiled and touched her hair with her finger tips, so as not to mess it. "I'll expect you girls in bed early," she said, and went down the steps.

Chloris made a face. She waited till Mom was down in the living room. "What time is he coming over?" she whispered.

I shook my head. "I don't know."

"Don't you know anything?"

We heard a car coming up the canyon road. We looked out her window and saw the headlights turn into our driveway.

"I'm hungry," Chloris said. "I'm going down for a snack."

"Me, too," I said, and followed her down.

We had the refrigerator open and began taking things out. A million things we didn't intend to eat. Mom heard us and got up from the sofa. She was about to say something when the door chimes sounded. She hurried for the door, smoothing down her skirt.

We heard her say, "Come in, Duane. I see you found it, all right."

"No problem," he said.

Mom saw us both standing there, between the dining and living room, holding plates with ice cream and cookies.

"These are my daughters. Say hello to Mr. Turner, girls."

"Hi."

He was much younger than Fidel. I saw that right away. Tall and slightly bald with light frizzy blonde hair, what there was of it. He looked kind of flabby and pale. He was dressed in a sharp business suit, with a striped shirt and dark tie. I didn't like his type at all.

181

"The older one is Chloris. The other is Jennifer."

Chloris said, "Hello, Mr. Turner."

I looked. She was smiling up at him. I nearly dropped dead. No mumble, no dirty look, no creep talk—*hello, Mr. Turner!*

Mom noticed it and looked surprised and pleased. There was no way she could forget how rude Chloris had been to her men friend visitors.

"Mr. Turner is a business acquaintance," Mom said lightly. "His company puts out some very good products that we use at Bontel's."

Chloris cut in. "Like what kind, Mr. Turner?"

He smiled down at her. "The cosmetic line, Chloris. Lipstick and powder, hand lotions. Bath soaps, colognes."

"Gy!" she said, looking wide-eyed and impressed.

"If you like, maybe I'll have some sent over—for you girls. We have a 'young miss' line, too."

"Wonderful," Chloris said. "Thanks a lot."

I didn't say anything. Suddenly, it seemed as if Chloris and I had switched personalities. She was being me, gushy and friendly, and I was being a sullen goon, like she usually was.

"Well, say good night, girls," Mom said. "You can take what you're eating upstairs with you."

That shook me up, too. If Mom had one rule you couldn't break, it was taking food to your room.

182

"Good night, Mr. Turner," Chloris said. "Nice meeting you."

"Yeah," I said, turning away.

"Night," he said. As we left, I heard him say to Mom. "Nice girls you have, Marge." Not Margaret. *Marge!*

We went back to the dining room to get our plates. On the way out and upstairs, I peeked inside. Mr. Turner was sitting on the sofa next to Mom. He looked too soft and comfortable, sitting half-facing her with one arm over the top of the sofa. He wasn't sitting on the big side chair.

He wasn't any dummy.

Mom had the stereo on playing soft music. I followed Chloris upstairs.

"He's nice," she said. She didn't whisper it. It was almost as if she wished they could hear it downstairs.

"He's a creep," I said.

I heard myself say it, too late. I opened my mouth to change it, say something else, but Chloris hadn't missed it. She smiled, and went into her room.

I stomped into mine, making more noise than usual. I shut my door hard and turned on my TV. Then I sat down and looked at what I had brought up to eat. I didn't have any appetite. I turned my TV low, opened my door slightly, and listened. I could hear the stereo music going. Once in a while, the sound of their voices. Then a period of silence with just the soft music.

Chloris had her record player on. Her door was shut tight, as if she didn't care what was happening downstairs with Mom and her business acquaintance visitor.

I closed my door again. I turned my TV sound up and lay down on my bed to watch it. I watched it for an hour without any interest. It was the dumbest TV program I'd ever seen.

I turned it off, got undressed, put out my light and tried to sleep. I couldn't. Usually I'm a perfect sleeper.

I looked at my clock. Ten to 12:00, it said. I opened my door quietly. Chloris had her lights out, her door shut. I heard soft music coming from the living room. I closed my door and crawled back into bed.

When Fidel was home, Mom always went to bed early, around 9:30, 10:00. She was always sleepy and tired. Exhausted, she would sometimes say.

I didn't like this. I didn't like the way Mom seemed so friendly and at ease with Mr. Turner. I wondered how well she knew him, and then suddenly I wondered if he was the reason Mom had been missing dinners with us lately, that working-late-jazz.

I wished Fidel would hurry home.

184

I must have fallen asleep because I never heard Mr. Turner's car drive away from our house. I went to the door, opened it and listened. There wasn't any more music. It was dark downstairs.

I cried myself to sleep. I hadn't done that since I was a baby.

21

Mom was cheerful the next morning at breakfast. Before she left for work, she said, "Well, how did you like Mr. Turner?"

I shrugged. "He's okay, I guess."

"He's very intelligent," Mom said. "Quite successful for a young man."

"How come you're seeing him?" I said. "I mean, how come he came over here?"

Mom lost a lot of that cheery smile. "What do you mean?" she said sharply. "I told you he was a friend. I have a right to have my friends visit me at my own home, don't I?"

I nodded. "Yeah, I guess."

"Anyway," Mom said. "Did you notice—Chloris seemed to like him?"

"Yeah, I noticed."

"That's an encouraging sign," Mom said. "I must tell Dr. Smythe about that at our next appointment."

After she left for work, I got the newspaper. I looked at Mom's horoscope right away. TAURUS: *Study new ways to expand in the near future and*

186

*free yourself of obstacles to progress. Discuss plans
with those who can help.*

I felt like throwing up.

Mine was weird again. LIBRA: *Study new philos-
ophies to make your life richer and more as you
want it. Correspondence and long distance calls
could be profitable.*

Chloris had another good one. SCORPIO: *Come
to a better understanding with others who are vital
to your plan of life. Be optimistic.*

Finally, I read Fidel's. MOON CHILDREN: *Keep
promises you have made to others which are valid.
Then later you can have a fine time with the one
you love. Be considerate.*

I knew Fidel was patient. Well, he would have
to stay with it, and hope for the best. I wished
Mom had his forecast because she was the one
who seemed to need it. Mr. Wood was sure screw-
ing up our family. I hoped he would rush a reply
to my letter. I had given everybody's birth signs
and explained the situation.

Kathy wasn't too cheerful at the bus stop or
on the ride. She asked me what Mr. Turner was
like. "He's a cosmetic freak," I told her.

The kid who liked to pull our hair sat at the
other end of the bus, ignoring us. "I'm beginning
to miss it already," Kathy said. "That boy was
the only one who related to me on this dumb bus."

Mr. Farrell looked terrible. His face was puffy,

his eyes red-rimmed. "I really tied one on last night," he said. "I hope none of you kids ever gets married. Marriage is very unscientific."

I told him this day correspondence and long distance calls could be profitable.

"You got to be kidding," Mr. Farrell said. "I can't even pay last month's phone bill."

"What about correspondence?" I said.

"I don't know anybody. My wife is the only one I know and she won't talk to me."

"Maybe you could send her a letter."

"I don't think my wife knows how to read."

I told him from now on I would tell him what his stars had in store for him, as my Libra forecasts were the same as his.

"I don't put too much stock in that stuff," he said. "The great Paracelsus once said: 'Constellations are subordinate to the wise man. They have to follow him, not vice versa. Only a man on the animalistic level is ruled by the planets. Just as a thief cannot escape the gallows, a murderer cannot escape hanging.'"

"What does that mean?" I said.

Mr. Farrell rubbed his eyes and tried getting them to focus. "It means I'm a dead duck. When my wife gets me into court, besides everything else, I'm willing to bet she gets custody of our color TV."

He sank back in his chair, waved his hand and

188

told us we all could do whatever we wanted again. Not too many wanted that.

On the way back, Kathy talked about her mother's new date. "He looks like he just got out of college. I think he's younger than she is. How about your mother's friend, that Duane Turner?"

"I think they're almost the same age."

"How old did you say Fidel was?"

"About 60. He's in good shape, though."

"Rotsa ruck," Kathy said.

Mom called later to say she wouldn't be home for dinner, she had some inventory to do. She told me we should use up the rest of the hamburger meat. I said, "Have a good time."

"I told you I have inventory work to do," she said crossly.

"Well, yeah, that's what I meant." After hanging up, I told myself, *like fun you did!*

Chloris didn't look surprised when I told her Mom would be working late at the store. "That figures," she said.

"She said she's got all that inventory to do."

Chloris nodded. "Yeah, I'll bet," she said sarcastically.

"What's inventory mean?"

She asked, didn't I know anything? I shook my head, no. "It means," Chloris said, "where you have to do that stuff that's around there."

Chloris made the hamburgers that night. They

189

didn't taste any better than Mom's. Chloris wolfed hers down.

"Now, this is what I call a terrific hamburger," she said. "Don't you notice the difference?"

I told her I didn't.

"You're too young to know the difference," she said. "When you get older, it unlocks that gourmet part of your brain."

We sat around and watched TV and did our homework and had a late snack, and then another later one after that. Some tarts with fruit on top and ice cream.

We were in bed when Mom came home. It was a quarter to 11:00. I heard her humming a tune when she came up the steps.

Maybe that inventory isn't so tough to do, after all, I thought.

22

Mr. Wood nearly threw me Wednesday.

LIBRA: *You can get those duties done in jig time now that you are feeling stronger. Search for a new big car you want, or fine apparel.*

I felt like yelling at him, Help, you got it all wrong! I'm only 12 years old. How am I going to get a new car? I remembered what Mr. Farrell had told me about not being able to pay his last telephone bill. He also couldn't afford any new big car. Not fine apparel, either, unless he found some in a thrift shop.

I decided it had to be the secretary's fault. She was in love with some freaky guy who was sapping her mind.

Mom's nearly gave me an ulcer. TAURUS: *If you are friendly with others, you find they give you the support you need at this time. Accept invitations. Get rid of opposition quietly and expertly.*

Chloris had another one perfect for her. SCORPIO: *Contact individuals who give you good advice. Arrange now for that important change you want to make. Spend evening with family at home.*

At breakfast, I asked Mom when Fidel was coming home. She thought, perhaps, Friday. I asked if she had called him up there about his new show. She said, no, she hadn't. She'd been awfully busy. I asked if Mr. Turner was coming over again.

"I don't know at the moment," Mom said. "Why are you so interested in Mr. Turner?"

"I don't know. I guess because he's your friend."

"Yes. He's helped me a lot in my new job, too. I didn't know the first thing about being a buyer."

"Is he married?"

Mom studied me. "No, he's divorced."

"About how old would you say he was?"

Mom flipped then. "That's enough, now! I don't know how old he is, and I don't care. If you really want to know, ask him next time he's over. I've had enough with your questions, Jenny. Fidel's away and I don't like being alone evenings. Now eat your breakfast and don't bother me. I'm late for work."

"Okay," I said. "How did the inventory work out?"

"It worked out fine. Anything else?"

"You working late again tonight?" I wanted to add we didn't like to be alone evenings, either.

"No," she said. "Anyway, I don't think so. But I only work there. If they ask me to help out, I have to do what they say."

192

I said goodbye. I wished I knew what was going on inside her head.

Kathy had a letter from her father in Texas. "He told me everything was fine. It was a good company and they liked his work. He said he hoped I was coming along okay, and missed him." She stopped, tears in her eyes. "Would you believe such a dumbbell for a father? He didn't say he missed me, only did I miss him."

"Maybe he left that out because he didn't want to make you cry," I said.

Kathy burst into tears. "He sure did a good job."

The kid who pulled hair wasn't on the bus.

"Gosh, I hope nothing's wrong with that boy," Kathy said. "Maybe I hit him too hard on the head with those books."

"Well, you had to, he was pulling your hair."

She thought about it. "Maybe next time, I'll use only one."

Mr. Farrell looked worse than ever. He forgot to shave, his eyes were bleary, bloodshot, and had bags under them. His clothes looked like he slept outside on the lawn.

"I think I know what's bugging my wife. Like every difficult problem, the answer is really simple."

"Okay. What?"

"She doesn't like me."

"You're kidding."

"No, I don't think she ever did."

"Then why did she marry you?"

"For spite, I guess. That, and she knew I had this color TV set." He rubbed his jaw. "What's in my stars today?"

I told him Mr. Wood's exact words. That he could get his duties done in jig time now that he was feeling stronger. And he could start searching for a new big car, or buy some fine apparel.

Mr. Farrell thought about it and fumbled for a cigarette in the crumpled package on his desk. "Maybe. No question about the fact I'm feeling stronger. Did he say what make or model to buy? I don't have any opinions about that."

"No, he left that up to us."

He reached into his pocket and came up with a few soggy bills. "I've got three dollars and some change. Maybe you're the one who's loaded."

I told him I was broke, too.

Mr. Farrell sighed and lit his cigarette with a shaking hand. "Okay. Anything else?"

"Yeah. You're not allowed to smoke in classroom."

Mr. Farrell shook his head in disagreement. "It didn't say I couldn't in my forecast."

"Come on, Mr. Farrell," I pleaded. "Put it out. You'll get fired."

"Swell," he said. "Less alimony."

He fell asleep then with the cigarette in his mouth, and we all did what we wanted to again.

194

The kid whose father was a TV dealer said he was going to report Mr. Farrell for smoking in class. I asked him what his sign was. Scorpio, he said.

I should have known.

Mom called a little while after I got home. She said she was sorry, but she had to work late again. There was a mix-up, she said, on some orders and she had to go through the whole damn mess to get it straightened out. She said she'd be home as soon as she could. And we should use up the rest of the hamburger meat.

"We did that last night," I said.

"Well, then, scramble some eggs. Eggs are very nutritious."

"I had eggs for breakfast."

"Maybe there's some tuna. You could make a tuna salad."

I told her okay, we'd work up something.

Chloris wasn't upset. She liked tuna anyway. "She's sure got a rough job. I hope they pay her a lot for all that overtime." She smiled sweetly. "Maybe Duane will buy her a nice dinner."

After dinner, she went up to her room and closed her door.

She put up the sign:

NO ADMITENCE. THIS MEENS YOU.

I remembered this was another night for her to be in touch with those individuals for advice.

Arranging for the important change she wanted to make.

Mr. Wood made it easy for her, too, telling her she should spend the evening at home. She never went anywhere, anyhow.

Fidel called from San Francisco. I answered it. Chloris ducked back inside her room when she heard me mention his name. He asked if Mom was home so he could speak to her. I told him she was working on some mix-up at the store. He asked me how I was. I told him fine. I asked about his show. He said so far he hadn't sold anything, but a few people were interested. He said he'd be home by Friday, and to stay well.

The phone rang again. Chloris let me go for it. With her Scorpio power over me, I did it, too. I said hello and then called her. "It's for you."

She stood in her doorway, questioning silently. "Who is it?"

"Alice Packer."

Chloris covered the phone, whispering. "I hope she's not too upset about losing Rick." She picked up the phone and began talking, using that phony charm and eagerness she puts on at times. "You don't tell me," she said, after a while. She listened and then said, "Well, sure, that's swell, Alice . . . honest . . . no, no thanks . . . I wouldn't . . . " She kept on like that, buttering Alice up, and then said she had to go now, and hung up.

She saw my questioning look, and shrugged, curling her lip. "Who needs him? He's a freak anyway. I told you."

"What happened?"

"She called to tell me Rick Harrison was taking her to a party Saturday night. She asked if I wanted her to get me a date . . . can you imagine?"

"But you told me Rick told you he gave her up."

Chloris frowned and narrowed her eyes. "Well, that's what I mean about those freaky ones. You can't ever trust them!"

She slammed her door behind her and tuned her radio up loud. I went to my room and got with George Washington again. He must have had a rotten orthodontist, because they had him wearing *wooden* teeth.

Mom came home at 10:15. She wasn't humming. Her feet were dragging. Mix-ups are harder on you than inventory.

23

Chloris was sleeping soundly next morning. The tape recorder was on the floor near her bed. I watched the tapes spinning. I didn't hear Daddy's spirit saying anything. Unless it was in a language I couldn't hear.

Mom left early before I had a chance to talk to her at breakfast. I scrambled my egg, made toast and drank some milk. I didn't feel so good. I felt all shaky inside.

There was a letter in our mail box, marked SPECIAL DELIVERY. It was addressed to Mr. Gene Carpenter. That dopey secretary Mr. Wood had couldn't read my handwriting. I opened his letter trying hard not to be nervous. *It's what you wanted,* I told myself.

Dear Friend:

As a rule, we do not reply to personal problems. But your letter indicated how troubled you are, and therefore we are answering your request.

For the LIBRA native, there are great difficulties ahead. Saturn is sitting on your Moon. This is temporary, as Saturn is in transit. You will have good health. Venus is well aspected, denoting efficient kidneys, and therefore the power to rid the body of poisons easily.

The TAURUS sign will undergo great change. There will be a distinct break with the past. Uranus in Scorpio.

The CANCER sign. Mars in the Eighth House, signifies quick end to a partnership. Moon in the Seventh House suggests fickle partner who needs companionship.

For SCORPIO, Uranus in the Third House suggests an unusual estrangement. Jupiter in the Second House suggests a tendency to exploit others. Gemini on the seventh cusp indicates that outside influence may interfere with this native's perspective.

Finally you ask if I think TAURUS will do something dumb. We have a variety of moral standards conflicting her judgment, (Saturn square Neptune) plus a vigorous desire (Mars conjunct Uranus trine Saturn) to escape from the sordid side of life (Pisces). Also Mars in Pisces quincunx Neptune does not help permanent relationships with the opposite sex. Further, Saturn shows by its afflicted position the native has been faced with problems of self-discipline. Saturn-Neptune square indicates a considerable element of desperation.

Remember, the stars foretell, they do not compel.

Astrologically yours,
Wilson W. Wood

I called Kathy right away. She said not to believe him. He hadn't done anything right yet.

I said I felt like cutting school. She said so did she, but what good would that do? So we went.

The school bus driver, Mr. Williams, was very red-eyed and happy. He said his wife gave birth early that morning to an 8-pound baby boy. He had some cigars in his shirt pocket and kept asking the kids if they were sure they didn't want any.

We all turned him down but saw he was kind of unsteady at the wheel this morning. So we just sat watchful and tense, telling Mr. Williams when a car was pulling out of a driveway ahead, in case he didn't notice it.

Mr. Farrell looked terrible again, more red-eyed than Mr. Williams. His hands were shaking, he needed a shave, and his breath had even more vodka on it than Mr. Williams'.

"I just got a note from the astrologer, Mr. Wood," I told him. "Saturn is sitting on our Moon. Things will be difficult for us Libras."

"You're telling me," he said. "I heard from my wife's attorney. They're asking for everything but my Spider plant."

"Can't you tell them you're broke?" I said.

Mr. Farrell waved his finger in front of his face. "That's a word you can't use with attorneys. It costs $500 to talk to them before you can tell them you're broke."

200

"Well, doesn't your wife know you're broke?"

"I've been trying to break the news to her for the past five years. But she never liked to discuss money. Not till now, that is."

Then he called the class to order and asked if anybody felt like discussing CNO Isotopes in the Interstellar Medium and Their Implications to Theories of the Chemical Evolution of the Galaxies.

Nobody volunteered. Mr. Farrell rocked back on his chair, looking us over moodily. "You're all chicken," he said.

The door opened and a kid came in. He waved a slip of paper at Mr. Farrell. "There's a phone call in the front office for you, if you want to take it. They said it was important."

Mr. Farrell sat thinking about it. The boy standing at the door got nervous. Mr. Farrell stood up and winced, then held on to his desk. "Ten to one, now they want my Spider plant," he said. He followed the kid out the door, shaking his head slowly. He was really walking funny.

Some of the kids laughed. "Boy, is he potted!" the TV man's kid said. Kathy and I looked at each other, worried.

After a while, Mr. Albee, the assistant principal came in. He told us Mr. Farrell had to leave on a pressing business matter, and we could use the remaining time for study or reading.

"Do you think he had to go downtown to meet with her lawyer?" I asked Kathy.

She shrugged. "Either that, or to get his plant ready."

A new driver was on the school bus for the ride back instead of Mr. Williams. He didn't know all the canyon stops and the kids caught on fast. They began jumping up to get off and making him jam on his brakes. After a while, he got mad and told us to cut it out or he'd make us all walk home.

Getting off, Kathy asked him what happened to our regular driver, Mr. Williams. He leaned toward her grinning. "Confidentially, kid, I hear old Williams had a snootful. They sent him home to sober up."

It was that kind of a day, weird things happening, like everybody was suddenly cracking up. I had to figure Uranus was at fault. That crazy planet of change.

I was too worried and nervous to go home. Kathy's mother was out shopping and we had cookies and milk, and listened to some of her records. Neither of us felt like talking about what was really on our minds. So we talked about everything else but. At 5:00, I got up to leave.

"You can stay here and have dinner with us, if you like," Kathy said.

I told her I better not, that I better get on home in case something was happening. So there it was,

202

the words falling out by themselves, and I left feeling depressed all over again.

Mrs. Kingman was heading into her driveway when I came out the door. She waved to me and gave me a big hello. She got out of her car carrying a lot of expensive looking department store packages.

I couldn't help noticing Kathy's mother looked awfully happy for a divorcing woman. It gave me something else to think about. I mean, did I want my Mom to be happy or not, if she intended to break up with Fidel.

I decided it was another thing I better not think about.

24

"What's keeping her this time?" Chloris said. "I'm hungry."

"Maybe she got tied up in traffic," I said. It was 6:30 and Mom was a half hour late already. I didn't care too much about dinner. My stomach felt rocky.

A car roared up the canyon and turned into our driveway. Chloris leaped up. "It's about time," she said and ran out of her room.

The front door opened and Fidel came in. Chloris stopped short near the top of the steps. Her lip curled. "Oh, it's *him!*" She retreated back into her room, slamming the door.

Fidel looked tired as if he had been driving all the way. The stubble of his beard rubbed against my cheek as he leaned down to hug me. He took a step back, his eyes happy. "You're looking real good. Some day I'll have to do a painting of you."

"No kidding?"

"No kidding. If I can just catch that big happy smile on your face." He looked around. "Mother not home yet?"

I shook my head. I grabbed his big hand and swung it. "What happened up there? Did you sell a lot of stuff?"

He looked down at me as if I was daft. "Are you kidding? You know, those big pieces I do cost an awful lot of money. It's not like selling hot dogs."

"Okay. Did you sell some?"

He grinned. "I sold one."

I clapped my hands. "Wow! That's terrific! How much?"

He shook his head in mock disapproval. "Money isn't that important, you know. It's the idea of—"

I cut him off, I was so excited. "I know. How much?"

He was teasing and had the folded check out of his shirt pocket. He snapped it open in front of my eyes.

I blinked. "Thirteen thousand dollars! Wow! How neat!" He watched me, amused, as I danced around the room waving the check. "Just think, Fidel—what if you sell all the others? We'll be rich."

He grimaced wryly. "Don't count on it. But maybe I'll sell another one or maybe two, if I'm lucky. The show has a whole month yet to run."

"You'll sell them all," I said. "You'll see. Which one did they buy?"

"The one you shined for me—naturally."

I danced back and gave him his check. "You see? Maybe we oughta go into business together."

He nodded and put the check back into his pocket. "I'd better think about that. Maybe you bring me luck."

"No maybe about it," I said. "You know I do."

The telephone rang and I jumped. It was Mom.

"I still have a lot of work to clear up," she said, "and I won't be home for a few hours. There are some TV dinners for you and your sister in the freezer."

"Fidel's home," I said. "Don't you want to talk to him?"

"I don't have time," Mom said. "I'll see him later."

She hung up before I could say anything else. Fidel had started for the phone and then stopped. "It was Mom," I told him. "She said she couldn't talk to you now, but she'll be home in a few hours. She has to work."

He nodded, looking disappointed.

"We got some TV dinners to heat up. Would you like one, Fidel?" I said.

He shook his head and turned away. "Thank you, I'm not hungry."

"She's been working awful hard at her place. That new job she took over must be tough."

"Yes," he said. "When they give you more money, you have to work for it." He patted my head. "You'll be all right? You can fix your own dinner?"

"Oh, sure. All you do is heat it."

"Fine," he said. "I'll see you later."

He went out the side door toward his studio. I called Chloris and told her the good news about the TV dinner.

"That's a fine time to call and tell us," she said. "Now I lost my appetite."

She ate all of hers and part of mine. We watched TV a while and then went upstairs. Fidel was still working in his studio.

He was using his electric hand saw. It has such a weird sound, like a person crying in pain. It always gives me the shivers. I like it a lot more when he's hammering things.

I told Chloris about Fidel selling his statue for $13,000.

She turned up her nose. "Big deal."

"Well, it is," I said, annoyed. "Thirteen thousand dollars is a lot of money."

"It's not so much," she said. "You couldn't even buy a Rolls Royce with it."

I got bored with her after that and went back to my own room. I watched my own TV set a while, then turned it off and read. I kept an ear open for Mom coming home but the sounds on the canyon road were other cars zipping along. Finally I couldn't keep my eyes open any longer.

It was 10:00 when I put out my light. I left my door open so I could hear when Mom came home.

I was having a real wild dream. People were chasing me all over the place, yelling at me. I tried to tell them I hadn't done anything but they didn't want to listen. They kept coming after me throwing things and I finally had run out of breath and had to find a place to hide. The only place I could find was Bontel's Department Store, where Mom worked.

She looked at me unsmiling. "What are you doing here? Why aren't you in bed?"

I tried to explain but she wouldn't listen either. Her voice got louder. I woke up and it was Mom talking downstairs.

I was still sweating from that hairy dream, but I was so glad she was home, I forgot all about it. I hopped out of bed. Chloris had her door closed and her light was out. The living room lights were on downstairs. I heard Mom's voice, flat and harsh, her ordeal voice, and I felt my heart thumping in my chest, and crept down the steps to listen.

"Stop saying it's my job," she said. "It's not my job. I like my job."

"Then what is it?" Fidel said.

"It's us," Mom said. "It's you and me."

Get ready, I told myself. Here it comes. That rotten Uranus in Scorpio. Taurus breaking with the past.

"Perhaps we should discuss this another time,"

Fidel said. "You're tired now, Margaret, and —"

"No. I think we might as well get it over with now. I didn't plan it this way, either, for a surprise when you got back. But these past few days that you've been away have given me time to think. To see things clearly about our relationship."

Fidel laughed softly. "I have the feeling I've heard this speech somewhere before. Or is the TV set on?"

"I'm glad you're able to joke about it," Mom said. "Because I'm talking about wanting a divorce."

Her words hung there in the silence of the room. I had the feeling that if I went down there, I could see them in the air like an animated sign blinking on and off. I leaned against the wall, closing my eyes. Oh, Mom, I thought, did you have to? What are you doing?

It had to be up to Fidel and his good nature now, I knew. Come on, Fidel, I urged silently, talk her out of it. Make her laugh. You know how to do that. Show her that check you got. Don't believe her. She doesn't know what she's saying . . .

It was like the dream. Nobody was listening to me.

"This is a surprise, all right," Fidel murmured. "When did you make up your mind?"

"Look," Mom said. "I don't like going through this any more than you do. I don't know when

I made up my mind. Maybe when I got tired of your neglecting me, taking me for granted. When I realized I'm not happy living this way with you, knowing you don't really love me."

I was inching down the steps. I had to see them now. They were sitting at opposite ends of the big sofa with more space between them there than I'd ever seen. Mom looked pale, and angry. She twisted and rubbed her hands in her lap.

"I'm sorry to have been neglecting you," Fidel was saying. He had lost the happy good-natured expression I was used to seeing. He lit his pipe, puffed on it, threw down the match and rumpled his thick hair. "But so far as loving you —"

"My mind's made up," Mom said doggedly. "I'm not going to change it."

"I remember now what you told me about your first husband. He neglected you, you said. He didn't love you, you decided. This sounds like a familiar pattern."

"There's no comparison between you and my other husband," Mom said sharply. "He failed me in his own way."

Fidel nodded and puffed on his pipe. "I suppose I should have known. The signs were there. You've been nervous, jumpy —"

"If the signs were there, you put them there," Mom said. "You're always working. You never have the time to talk to me, to be with me. I want more out of a marriage than that."

210

"For example?" Fidel said, calmly puffing.

"I don't have to give you a list," Mom said. "All I know is that now I'm looking toward the future. My future. Your work is obviously more important to you. That's fine with me, and I'll make my life elsewhere."

Fidel tapped out his pipe. "I thought from the beginning that you understood my way of life, my work—"

Mom cut him off, angrily swinging her leg. "Maybe I did, but I've changed. I've met another man recently. He relates more to what I want from life. We enjoy each other's company. We talk to each other, have things to say—things in common. It just so happens that he's connected with my business at the store."

Fidel nodded. "I agree being able to talk to somebody, to exchange views, is important. But I think love is even more important. I thought we loved each other. Do you love this man?"

Mom shrugged and pushed her hair back. "I don't know yet. It might work out that way. He's not somebody I've met who's swept me off my feet, if that's what you're suggesting. No, I wouldn't call it love, exactly.

"But I didn't love my first husband that much either, at first. There was another boy before him I was mad about. We met at school, and he was my first real love. His parents were very wealthy—an old Pasadena family. I thought we would get married but his parents wanted him to establish his business career first. He listened to them—and I lost him."

Mom went on, her voice flat and unemotional, as if she was talking things over with a clerk at the supermarket. "Then I began going with Larry. I didn't have the same feeling for him that I had for Bob, but Larry was interesting and fun to be with. So we dated, there wasn't anybody else, and we got married. Our marriage lasted ten years. After a while, I loved him very much. But he changed toward me, became more distant, less loving—I felt I was alone—"

"You're a grown woman, Margaret, with two daughters—and still you want somebody to hold your hand? To tell you every minute how wonderful you are?"

"You're damn right," Mom said, grimly. "I'm not happy with you, and I'm not going to hang around waiting for you to change. It's my life and I intend to live every minute of it, the way I want to live it."

Fidel said slowly, "You're free to do as you wish. But you make a decision you have to be responsible for, Margaret."

"What the hell does that mean? Am I responsible for your being an artist? Wanting to be by yourself, to create your things—your masterpieces?"

Chloris was walking softly down the steps. She

saw me crouched near the bottom. She sat down a few steps above me, giving me a knowing malicious smile.

She must have heard all of it, I thought. But now it didn't matter who heard what.

I knew finally what had been on Mom's mind. What was eating away at her inside, making her so nervous. And my sister Chloris was right. She knew all the time.

Or maybe, I thought, she was only wishing, and made it come true.

I focused my blurred eyes on Fidel now.

"There is Jenny to consider," Fidel said. "You must know she loves me, has accepted me as her father. We love each other. I feel as if she is my own daughter."

"Well, that's unfortunate," Mom said. "I can't put an end to my life because of that. She might get to like this other man I know. Chloris seems to like him. Do you realize what that means? She never accepted you. Perhaps we might have a normal family again. She might become friendly with me again, love me as she used to before her father died. If you care to have Jenny visit with you sometimes, I won't stand in your way."

"Thank you, Margaret. I'm sorry I failed you. I hope you have better luck with your new life."

He walked out. I ran out the side door and found him in his studio. I ran to him.

"You didn't do those things you said. You let

her say all those mean things to you. You didn't fight back."

"Mr. Nice Guy?" Fidel said. "Yes, I did not fight back and it is wrong. But then, her mind was made up and you cannot change a person's mind to think your way. Also I am too old to change my own ways and habits. A sensible man must consider whether the situation is worth fighting for. If she wants another man. I cannot stop her. I am sorry for you. I hope you will be happy."

"He's a business freak," I said wildly. "He's younger than you. That's why she's doing it. He's a big bald nothing!"

"No, you are wrong," Fidel said. "Being young is something, not nothing. He has more life to give to your mother. A man nearer her age would be better, you see. They could live their natural span out together. What if I were to die in a few years? Then she is middle-aged, with two children, and it would not be so easy for her to find a husband. No, better for her now, while she is still young and attractive enough."

I held on to him. "I don't like her now."

He smoothed my hair. "Time is all that matters. It will be all right." He dried my eyes. "The other day we talked of forgiving. Do you remember?"

25

We moved back to another apartment in West-wood. It was like living back in the city. I hated it. I missed the trees and the mountains behind the house in the canyon, the crazy night birds chattering away, asking each other what happened, sending regards to relatives.

Westwood was closer to Beverly Hills, an easier drive to work for Mom. A week after we moved in, as she was leaving for shopping, she told me Mr. Turner would be over in the evening for dinner.

I shrugged. After all, I didn't pick him.

When Chloris came down, I told her about it. "Duane Turner. Remember him? He's coming for dinner with us. Maybe you'll get a chance to sit next to him."

Chloris twisted her lip. "Me? Sit next to that creep? Are you kidding?"

I stared. "I thought you liked him. Even Mom thought—"

Chloris shook her head. "Me like that fat bald freak? No way." She shook her head back and forth, back and forth. "No, no way."

"I don't get it," I said.

"You're really dumb, Jen. Fidel was Plan A. Remember? Then there was the final phase, remember?"

I nodded dumbly, still not understanding.

"Well, dumbbell, this Duane Turner was what we needed for the final phase. He helped us get rid of Fidel. You see?"

"You mean, you only pretended to like him—?"

"Well, sure. He was just what we needed to end Plan A. Now we're into Plan B."

"Plan B?"

"Right. Now we got to get rid of this Duane Turner freak. Don't you get it? I got this all worked out with Daddy's spirit."

I guess I should have known all along. The fortune cookies at Tom Foo's Chinese restaurant had told me exactly what would happen. Chloris got her wish, after all. Mom, too. I could see where I would never want to eat at a Chinese restaurant again.

I felt sorry for Chloris. She was going to go through her whole life hung-up forever on her dream of our dead Daddy, living only in her imaginary world, believing he was still talking to her.

I went to my room feeling a hundred years old.

It was only another Saturday, I told myself.

Kathy called. She said she never felt worse in her life. She felt terrible. She asked me how I

216

was, how things were over at my place. The same,
I told her.

Terrible.